PHARAOH'S BRIDE

TARA JADESTONE

"To be among kings, one must accept the prospect of the death of one's name, soul, and body."

PART I.

"Neferkempi," the Pharaoh whispered into her long, silken black hair. Seeing her, for the first time beside him as his wife, reassured him that life was good. She stirred at the sound of his voice while the Pharaoh leaned back, gazing down at her. Neferkempi was not her real name -it was Aneksi- but the Pharaoh had given the name to her out of affection and it served as a constant and pleasant reminder about how they had fallen in love.

Aneksi used a hand to cover her blushing face after noticing that the Pharaoh was awake and watching her. He chuckled lightly at her behavior.

"How many more nights will it take to ease you out of your shyness?" he asked with a sleepy smile.

Aneksi brought her hand away from her face to watch the Pharaoh with adoration as he closed his eyes and shifted an arm around her waist to pull her in close. The Pharaoh was right -it was not their first night together- but Aneksi felt as if it were. Because now it was the cotton-spun sheets from the Palace that separated the two from the outside world, not the draperies from her father's Temple. How could she explain that to him?

Aneksi pressed her face against the groove of his neck and

shoulder, seeing the bright light of day through the curtained opening that led to their personal garden. Her face sobered.

Across from this chamber were the consort chambers. There, the pharaoh's five other wives had a place to themselves when they were not requested, but close enough to be called upon the Pharaoh's whim.

Within moments, Aneksi could feel the Pharaoh's breathing slow against her hair and his hold slacken. He was asleep again. Aneksi shook her head, giving the sleeping Pharaoh a smile and brushed her lips against his skin before slowly drawing herself away from him. Flipping over, Aneksi grabbed her clothes from the floor and dressed herself into them. The white cloth garment wrapped around her chest and body while also exposing her back. The material itself was extremely light, with even the slightest breeze feeling as if it touched her bare skin. But the months of Ra's intense light were upon them and the clothes brought comfort.

In the garden was a towering statue of a goddess on her knees, arms splayed out in flight, and her head turned up to stare at the changing sky. The statue was as real as one could be, with high cheekbones, grooved fingernails, carved strands to show windswept hair, and a perfectly rounded body. It stood above a three-foot marble pedestal and was surrounded by potted palms and ferns; a replica of the goddess Ma'at's altar from Aneksi's former residence with her father at the Tri-God Temple.

Aneksi dropped to her knees and bowed her head at the statue's base, feeling the sun beat bright and strong against her bare back.

"Oh, Ma'at, Goddess of Justice and Truth, I am but your loyal servant. I implore you to keep this great kingdom under your order and bless the Pharaoh with an eternal life of wisdom and compassion."

The rattle of a fallen jug rolling on the ground brought Aneksi out of her reverence to her patron goddess. She turned around at the noise with a hand on her chest, startled.

"Forgive me, Your Highness!" a male youth said in a hoarse whisper. "I didn't mean to!"

"Quite alright," Aneksi said with a nod. The boy bowed his head and stepped to grab the fallen jug. It had sustained a large crack along one of its sides. Aneksi wondered how the boy had gotten here, but waved away her doubt, assuming he was a servant with access to this part of the palace. "But if you will, do be careful around here. I would not want you waking the Pharaoh." The boy nodded solemnly at her words, holding the jug to his chest, before running off.

3

Some of the contents of the jug had spilled onto the ground, but Aneksi did not take heed of what it was. Instead, she stood up and walked out of the sunlight to enter back into the chamber. As she held the doorway's curtain up, a shaft of the sun's rays hit against the Pharaoh's shaven head, illuminating his face. When the curtain fell back, the room darkened once more.

Aneksi smiled at the still sleeping pharaoh and knelt at the side of the bed.

"It's time to rise," she whispered, using the back of her hand to stroke the Pharaoh's face. She watched his eyelids flicker and moved to withdraw her hand when he caught her wrist and brought her fingers to his lips. Aneksi shook her head, watching the Pharaoh now grasp her hand and lower it to his chest, over his heart.

"Let me enjoy this moment," he said at last.

"You should be enjoying the sun's warmth more," Aneksi amended, but could not help but settle down on the floor at his side. After all, they were ready to break away all tradition just days ago.

The Pharaoh opened his mouth to speak when the door to their private chamber swung open. It was followed by warning shouts from the guards.

Aneksi instantly broke away from the Pharaoh and stood up, eyes cast to the floor. With a frustrated sigh, the Pharaoh sat upright, hunched, and ran a hand over his bald head while he shifted to have the bed sheet cover his lower body. He blinked the sleep out of his eyes and glanced wearily at his First Wife, Kiya, who had dropped to her knees several feet away from the bed.

Her usual perfected face was smeared with black, green and gold- the leaking colors of her makeup. The veins of her eyes were a prominent red. Something had caused her great distress to have her appear before her Pharaoh as she was.

"What is it now?" he muttered, glancing away from her face. It was a distressing sight that reminded him too much of what he had left behind.

"Forgive me, but Her Grace insisted-" started one of the Pharaoh's personal guards. He glanced at Aneksi and then back to the Pharaoh.

"Oh, King of the Nile, Son of the gods, may you live on for an eternity, forgive my intrusion!" cried Lady Kiya, interrupting the fearful guard. "It is your son, Heir Prince Ankhetep! He does not rise from his sleep!"

The Pharaoh straightened at her words while Aneksi gasped, a hand over her chest.

"Is this true?"

Lady Kiya nodded. "Please! I ask that you see to our firstborn!"

The Pharaoh nodded solemnly.

"You may leave, First Wife. I will see our child."

Aneksi lowered her arm and clasped her hands together, twisting her fingers. Yes, she was indeed worried about the sudden occurrence that had befallen the young prince. But there was some sense of pain in her heart hearing the Pharaoh say such things to other women. But there was nothing she could do about it. 'Our child' did not involve her. It involved Lady Kiya. It involved Lady Ahset, Lady Akhara, Lady Meryt, and Lady Khemut. The five other wives of the Pharaoh who bore him children. Kiya also held the title 'First Wife' for being the mother to the Pharaoh's only son and Heir Prince.

Lady Kiya bowed her head and stood up from the floor. She glanced at Aneksi, and in that split second, Lady Kiya lowered her head and almost smiled, before exiting the chamber. Aneksi felt a chill run down her spine at the look she received and shivered in the heat.

The guards shuffled out behind Lady Kiya.

Once the door shut behind them, Aneksi turned to the Pharaoh. She watched him swing his legs down from the bed and grab his clothes from the bed-stand.

Aneksi exhaled lightly and began to walk out towards the garden. Perhaps it was best she stayed away while the Pharaoh dealt with personal affairs.

"Neferkempi," the Pharaoh said, looking over his shoulder, "come and dress me." Aneksi stopped walking and glanced at him, confused, while the Pharaoh shooed away a servant. Seeing that she had not yet come, the Pharaoh twisted his abdomen to face her more directly. "Why do you hesitate?" he asked, an eyebrow raised.

"I..." But she was at a loss for words. Servants usually dressed the Pharaoh; there was no need for her to do it.

"Come here, Neferkempi," he urged.

Aneksi quietly made her way over, standing before the Pharaoh. He gently placed his hands over her hips and stared up into her eyes. Aneksi could not help but feel his adoration towards her and she leaned forward in an instinctive manner, laying her hands on his shoulders.

"I know it will be difficult for you to become accustomed to this life," he said, catching her gaze. "But know that I did not bring you here to compare yourself to the women in this Palace." Aneksi's shoulders slumped and forced her eyes elsewhere, ashamed she was so easily read by the Pharaoh.

7

"Is it wrong of me to feel this way?" she whispered. "Perhaps if–" Aneksi stopped, feeling the Pharaoh's lips press against the fabric above her abdomen. Aneksi's eyes darted back to his, and he smiled up at her with softened eyes.

"Oh, Neferkempi, one day I shall be worrying about the health of our children."

PART II.

The Pharaoh watched as Aneksi smoothed down his robe with a smile and looked himself over in the stand-up mirror. He nodded his head in approval and then turned back to face Aneksi. He raised a hand and ran it through her hair. She closed her eyes and inclined her head as the Pharaoh leaned forward to gently kiss her forehead.

"Do not stray far," he said, dropping his hand to his side. He was smiling. "I'd rather not hear about you getting lost already." Aneksi nodded and the Pharaoh strode out of the room.

The Nursery was a circular chamber, supported by six columns painted with golden rings. Hieroglyphics of the god Bes lined the walls, the protector of infants and the young, and below them, stone bench seats were placed, decorated with cushions. At the center of the chamber was a small, but ornate imported ivory and marble bed, where the Prince Ankhetep slept. Just above the bed was a cut glass ceiling, allowing for Ra's light to shine directly down upon him.

At the Pharaoh's arrival, the servants formed a semi-circle around the Prince's bed with their heads bowed.

Lady Kiya did not react to the Pharaoh's presence, and instead, remained where she stood, staring mournfully at her son's sleeping face. The Pharaoh walked to her side and laid a hand briefly on her back. She turned to face him before falling to her knees.

"Please, O Grace of the Nile," she begged, clenching the bottom of his robe in her hands, "your son does not heed his mother's voice."

The Pharaoh glanced at Lady Kiya, grimacing, and then forced his eyes on the near-motionless boy before him. He leaned forward over the base of the bed, allowing the scene to sink into his heart.

"My son, Heir Prince Ankhetep, rise at the sound of your father's call," the Pharaoh said, reaching out to gently shake the child's arm.

There was no response.

The Pharaoh caught his breath, feeling his hope waver. "Ankhetep," he repeated, "your father calls you to rise."

Again, there was no response. Swallowing back the bile in his throat, the Pharaoh pulled back, feeling a sudden chill in the air. He turned to the servants. They shifted uneasily in their position. "Which of you were the first to notice the Prince's condition?" he demanded.

One of the women to the left took a small step forward. "It was I, your Greatness," she answered.

"And?" the Pharaoh asked, folding his arms across his chest. "What did you do?"

"I...I sent for the Prince's mother, Her Highness," she stuttered.

The Pharaoh turned his attention to his grieving wife, who remained at his feet. The Pharaoh felt a stab of pity for her in his chest but disregarded it. It was humiliating to have one of his wives shamelessly degrading herself before the servants, no matter the reason. And it was unlike the Kiya he knew to be such an emotional mess.

"First Wife, do not disgrace me by groveling on the floor." Kiya looked up at him, meeting his gaze with red-rimmed eyes. She rose to her feet slowly, accepting the Pharaoh's offered hand. "Now you," he said, facing the servants once more, "send for the High Priests and every notable physician of the Nile. I want this chamber to be filled with the men who can wake up my son." Several of the servants rushed to complete the task asked of them.

Once gone, Kiya wiped away the streaks of paints on her face with a kerchief a servant had passed to her and pressed against the Pharaoh's side.

"I pray Isis can guide our son to his former self," she whispered. The Pharaoh mutely nodded, unable to speak. He could not fathom how the child could have fallen ill. Ankhetep had always been a healthy, eccentric child.

Kiya made a move to draw the Pharaoh away from the bed but he brushed her hand away, not heeding her as he moved over to stand by the side of Ankhetep's bed. With a frown, Kiya walked out of the Nursery and did not look back.

The Pharaoh stared at Ankhetep's closed eyes, flaring nostrils, and closed mouth. His little Prince. The thought of losing such a treasure made the Pharaoh's eyes burn and tear up. Exhaling loudly, the Pharaoh composed himself, running a hand over his face. It was then, from the corner of his eye, did the Pharaoh notice something about the boy's face.

A dark shadow, serpent-like in form, glided below the Prince's skin. It made no protrusion as it slipped from Ankhetep's jaw to his temple.

The Pharaoh's hand fell to his side, breathless. Hoping he

had only seen a shadow of something above them, the Pharaoh turned up his head to look at the glass ceiling. But the sky was empty. The Pharaoh reached out a hand to touch Ankhetep's cheek and instantly drew his hand back.

The child's skin was burning hot.

"What are you doing, standing around here like beetles?" the Pharaoh shouted, sweeping his arm in frustration. The remaining servants perked up at his voice, their faces identical in fear at the tone of the Pharaoh's voice. "He is burning up and you keep him under the sun! Are you *trying* to kill him?" the Pharaoh shouted angrily, his knuckles white from gripping the bed's raised sides.

The servants leapt towards the Prince, picking him up from his bed and ushering out while the Pharaoh glared at the brilliant white linen blankets and bedsheets, his heart racing. What did he just see? Had an evil found a claim to his son's soul?

Aneksi could hear voices in the distance and the echo of the Pharaoh's commandeering voice. What they were saying, however, was inaudible to her. But she sat upright at the sound, having previously been draped across a lounge sofa with hands folded over her stomach.

Seeing that Aneksi was now sitting up, two nearby servants approached her and began to brush her hair.

Aneksi glanced at her childhood slave, Lithra, who was seated on the floor on the other end of the chamber. In front of her was a writing desk piled with books of all kinds and Aneksi did not know where she had gotten them.

But Aneksi also did not mind not knowing.

"Lithra, do you have any idea as to what is happening?" she asked.

The fair-skinned girl with blue eyes looked up from her reading. Her voice was monotone.

"Is it not His Excellency's son who has fallen ill? It will not be long before they call you in, Ani."

Aneksi furrowed her eyebrows.

"Call me in? What for?"

Lithra closed the book in front of her. Its cover was made of a thin layer of cowhide and it had the sewn imprint of an upside-down leaf.

"If they suspect the Prince's illness to be of unnatural causes, the entire Royal Family will be placed into confinement until the issue is addressed."

"Unnatural? You do not mean..." Lithra nodded. Aneksi gasped. "Who would dare poison a son of Ra? Oh, Ma'at, let it not be so!" Her slave remained quiet at this, turning to flip open to another book. Seeing her nonchalant reaction, Aneksi shook her head. "Yes, let us not think the worse. I pray that Prince Ankhetep will recover soon."

Lithra briefly looked up at Aneksi. Her expression was blank, but if you looked closely, which Aneksi did not, her eyes expressed annoyance.

"Of course, Ani. There is not a soul in these lands you wouldn't pray for." Aneksi smiled at these words, but Lithra had already turned her face away. Aneksi tilted her head, watching the older girl.

"Is there something wrong, Lithra?" she asked. "You haven't smiled once since we were situated in the Palace."

Lithra did not hesitate to answer. "I am still trying to find my place here. After all, I have only ever known was your father's Temple." Lithra had said the last two words with a grimace but the look quickly passed as she added, "How long has it been since the Pharaoh woke up, did you say? It must be time for you to ready yourself for breakfast."

PART III.

Behind the length of carved wood that made up the dining table, was the Pharaoh, seated upon a raised floor pillow made from goose feathers. He sat high upon the raised platform, by himself. Throughout the eight years in his reign, the political atmosphere brought every one of his wives up to sit beside him, though none of the Pharaoh's wives found it to be a permanent seat. Below the platform were stone steps, rounded off as semi-circles that wee covered in dark green rugs. Perpendicular to the platform was another long wooden table, set with today's breakfast. Chairs mirrored each side, numbering ten in total. On a normal day it would seat the Pharaoh's five wives on one side and the children he had with each, respectively, on the other side. Today, however, he would only see four of his children.

The Pharaoh did not have to wait long for his family to arrive. His wives entered in order of marriage date, with Ahset and Akhara arriving first, followed by their daughters Nebta, aged seven, and Hemetre, who was a few months younger than her sister. Then came his third wife, Meryt, and her daughter Thut. She was six. Khemut came in behind her, holding her daughter, Freyi's, hand. Freyi was five years old. The last of the five to enter was Kiya.

Like the other wives, her face had been perfected with powder gold and minerals. They all wore white cotton dress robes, gold necklaces, and a single gold band on their left arm to display their position as consorts. But unlike them, Kiya was, by far, the prettiest. A gift many attributed to her patron goddess, Isis. But the four other wives were not ill at ease; they knew it was Prince Ankhetep's ailing health -not herself- that had captured the Pharaoh's heart as his eyes lingered on Kiya more than usual. Aneksi arrived moments later. In an instant, the Pharaoh's eyes drew away from Kiya and his face lit up with a smile as Aneksi stepped out from behind her.

Aneksi's eyes were also painted, but having run late, she wore no powder on her face. Upon her head, she wore a bronze circlet, the symbol of her new status as the Pharaoh's consort, with beads and small jewels weaved into her braided hair. As a new bride, she wore a silken white dress, slit at the sides, and a bejeweled belt around her waist.

She turned her attention away from the Pharaoh to draw her eyes to the table. There was no extra chair set for her there. Aneksi looked back up at the Pharaoh, seeing that the Pharaoh's smile had gotten wider. He motioned for her to walk forward and take the seat beside him.

Aneksi hesitated. Lithra had told her that sitting next to Pharaoh in the public would have her equated to being Great Royal Wife. And since the Pharaoh still had not officially named which of his wives would be the one to take the title, it was something to be cautious of.

As she walked up the steps to sit at his side, Aneksi felt the cold stares of her fellow consorts and even some from the servants in the chamber. But the Pharaoh did not seem disturbed at all by their reactions. He had not once taken his gaze off her as she walked forward, and when Aneksi made it up to the last steps, the Pharaoh took hold of her hand and guided her to his side. Once Aneksi settled down onto the pillow, she received a sudden kiss on her cheek. Aneksi felt her face heat, refraining from looking in the Pharaoh's direction or at anyone else. How would the other wives react to his open affection?

What followed after was a moment of absolute silence. Aneksi's gaze moved from one consort's solemn face to another. Their demeanor did not express any vehemence, but neither did they seem all too welcoming of Aneksi. When her eyes landed on Kiya, Aneksi felt her heart stop for a second. The older woman's narrowed, dark eyes, pursed lips and lifted chin was of a look that far from being pleased.

The booming call from the Royal Master of Servants broke the tension in the air.

"Rise, for the Glorious Child of Ra, Son of the Great Amanrakh and grandson of the Fearless Tyamun, may their souls reach Anubis as rays of light and fire." The five wives of the Pharaoh stood by their seats in utmost stillness as he spoke, while the younger of the children fidgeted in their spot. "–the Ruler of the Nile and her reaches, may He live for an Eternity favored by the gods, and may He bless us with His wisdom so that the people of the Blacklands forget not to bow before Him in servitude." The Pharaoh raised his hand, indicating that they be seated. The servants walked forward and pulled the chairs out, allowing for each wife and daughter to take their seat.

Aneksi eyes flitted from one person to another, watching silently as everything happened like it did any other day for the others in the chamber. However, she felt alienated. Aneksi had anxiously listened to the Master of Servants, and watched to see if the other consorts said or did anything in particular for her to emulate. The procedure and rules of the Palace were still mostly unknown to her and a nervous tick made her leg involuntarily shake.

The Pharaoh placed his left hand on Aneksi's thigh and rubbed his thumb back and forth slowly along her exposed skin. Aneksi blinked out of her state and turned her head to the Pharaoh. He remained facing forward, but he smiled. Aneksi turned away and exhaled. She let it out slowly, squaring her shoulders. This would be the first of countless mornings for her in the Palace. She could not let her anxiousness get the better of her.

Water bowls were given first, to rinse one's hand for eating. Then came the platters of fruits and bread and jugs of water and beer. Throughout the breakfast, Aneksi nodded or smiled her thanks to the mute servants -one of whom was Lithra- as they refilled her cup or put another fruit upon her plate. Her mother had taught her it was a good gesture so they would trust their superiors. However, none of the servants met her gaze, and neither did any of the Pharaoh's other wives or their children, care to thank or acknowledge the servants. Aneksi wondered if no one else had been taught to do this by their mothers, or if such practices were simply not meant to be done in the Palace.

Sometime later, one of the Palace guards approached to speak to the Pharaoh. His wives, including Aneksi, all watched the Pharaoh as he leaned to his right to listen to the guard's message in private. His face remained emotionless for the few moments the guard spoke.

With a nod, the Pharaoh dismissed the guard back to his post and the meal resumed. Aneksi frowned at the Pharaoh's nonchalance, assuming that the guard had brought news regarding Prince Ankhetep's health. She received only a gentle pat on the knee from the Pharaoh in response.

It was not long before the meal was over. Servants began clearing away the remaining food and used plates. The Pharaoh held Aneksi's hand briefly once their silverware had been taken away, indicating that she follow him out of the dining chamber. As the two took a separate route only the Pharaoh was permitted to use, Aneksi straightened and glanced over her shoulder, feeling someone's stare on her back. And sure enough, where the other wives of the Pharaoh were being escorted back to their consort chambers, Kiya was scowling in her direction.

Aneksi froze at the spiteful look in Kiya's eyes.

"Neferkempi," the Pharaoh called, drawing Aneksi's attention back to him.

"Yes," she answered back, rushing to catch up with him.

The Pharaoh had reached their private garden, where he stood, leaning against one of the stone obelisks. Aneksi glanced over her shoulder again, seeing two Palace guards trailing behind them at a distance. She turned back to face the Pharaoh.

"What happened to your personal guards?" Aneksi asked, her eyebrows furrowed.

Lithra had mentioned that Palace guards were prohibited from leaving their post or route and that the Pharaoh was always surrounded by personal guards.

"I exiled them from the Palace. These two will be temporary guards of mine until I can find replacements," the Pharaoh shrugged.

"For what reason?" Aneksi raised her eyebrows. The Pharaoh looked over at her and took her hand.

"Because this morning their gaze never strayed from you," he said, bringing her hand to his lips. "I cannot trust them to keep me safe if they cannot recognize what is mine."

Aneksi stood silent in place, eyes wide and lips parted. Though she knew her father had power vested in him to do as he pleased, Aneksi could not fathom that their misplaced gaze had cost them their work. The Pharaoh smiled sheepishly at her confusion, his bronze-colored cheeks tinged red.

"Pharaoh—" she began.

"Neferkempi, what could possibly be wrong with me exiling them?" he cut in, holding onto her hand more tightly. His voice had become stern. "They could never fulfill their duty if they are distracted by you." His eyes followed her as she sat down by his feet, laying her free hand on his knee.

"And what if they had children," she whispered, breaking

his gaze to stare at the statue of Ma'at, "or unwell parents who depended on them? Without their service to you, their families have nothing to sustain themselves."

The Pharaoh followed her gaze, frowning. He turned back to Aneksi and tugged on her hand.

"Your words hold reason," he admitted. "But do you truly believe I have harmed them? That perhaps I may have caused a child to go hungry and grow hateful of their King? Or...or," Aneksi said nothing while he rambled on, "would this child of theirs remains ill as they have no means to purchase an antidote?" His eyes were distant and glittering as if he were to weep at any moment.

"How is the Prince?" she asked in a low voice, looking directly up into the Pharaoh's eyes. "Is his life so much in danger?" The Pharaoh's shoulders sagged. Aneksi patted his knee in comfort.

"Yes, I worry for his life," he whispered, closing his eyes. Aneksi sighed, seeing his eyelids flutter.

"I would tell you not to worry," Aneksi said with a slight laugh, "yet you prove to me time and again that your emotions precede reason when it is regarding those close to your heart." The Pharaoh opened his eyes to see Aneksi lean forward and peck his jaw. She smiled up at him, her hands on his knees. "But if you are to worry, let your tears fall. I see no wrong in weeping to ease your pain."

The Pharaoh's eyes narrowed but Aneksi held her gaze. A torn soul hidden behind a golden mask was the making of a tomb. Her mother was the reason she learned this at such a young age.

After a moment, the Pharaoh leaned forward and laid his forehead on hers. When they parted, Aneksi smiled through the wet streaks on her cheeks.

"Neferkempi," the Pharaoh said, watching as she stood up. Her smile grew wide at the adoration in his voice. He placed his arms around her waist and pulled her into an embrace. Aneksi closed her eyes and pressed her cheeks against the Pharaoh's chest, listening to the faint beat of his heart. "One can only thank the gods for having you."

PART IV.

"Ani- oh! Your Greatness!"

Lithra dropped to her knees. Her chin was pressed against her chest and her brown hair obscured her face from view. Aneksi turned around, stepping away from the Pharaoh to walk toward her slave.

"What is it that you want, Lithra?" Aneksi said, lifting

Lithra to her feet.

"It is nothing," she mumbled. Her eyes darted over Aneksi's shoulder and her fair skin quickly turned erubescent. The Pharaoh was smiling, his face radiating contentment. "It is nothing His Greatness' wife should ponder over."

"You needn't be so formal with me, but if you have nothing else to say, then you may go." Aneksi stepped back and Lithra nodded. She dipped her head once more in the Pharaoh's direction and rushed off.

Once gone, Aneksi placed her palm on the side of her forehead and blew out a sigh. Lithra's behavior was more than elusive the past months and her words sharp and careless. There had to be something wrong. But what? The Pharaoh stood up and took her hand.

"Neferkempi? What has upset you so quickly?" he asked.

"I...well it's Lithra," Aneksi said, her voice low. The Pharaoh raised an eyebrow, turning to look at the slave's retreating back.

"If she is no longer obedient, you can always give her away."

Aneksi shook her head. "No, it's not her obedience that is troubling me. She has become less than warm to me when we speak, alone or otherwise, for some time."

The Pharaoh let go of Aneksi's hand to flick her under the chin with his thumb. Aneksi tilted her head to a side, frowning the slightest at the Pharaoh's mocking gesture.

"You must realize a friendship between you and your servants is unnecessary," the Pharaoh said. "I would even say it is destructive."

"Why? I remember that my mother always told me to be kind to her. And Lithra has been nothing but good to me," Aneksi shot back in earnest, pleading with her eyes.

"I understand," the Pharaoh agreed, "but perhaps something has come between the two of you. But don't let it upset you so much. Why hurt yourself over it when it brings only more pain to those who see your hurting?"

"Well-" Aneksi started, but the Pharaoh shook his head.

"Neferkempi, your wellbeing is more important to me than any good slave. I was only allowed to take your slave out of the Tri-God temple's ownership because I argued with your father about how unhappy you would be in a foreign place with no one you knew. And look around you!" the Pharaoh made a sweeping gesture with his arm. "This garden, Neferkempi; I had it built to comfort you and your servant from being away from the only place you have ever lived. Have my efforts been in vain? Because here you are, hurting just the same as if you were alone." Aneksi opened her mouth and then closed it in concession. The Pharaoh gave her a small smile. "Lithra has a sound head and is dutiful. If you do not wish to keep her for any reason, I will ensure that she is received well by her next owner." He paused to add, "Who did you say she was from again?"

"A port merchant," Aneksi said, "who trades with the nations across the northern sea. She was an offering to my father when news of my mother falling ill had spread." Aneksi stopped to face the Pharaoh. His expression was somber. "But I do not want to give her away, not at all."

"Then make good use of her. She has only made you worry." Aneksi nodded, eyes downcast. "Do not give me such a sullen look. I will send for someone to fetch her. She may accompany us as we take a tour outside the Palace."

"Are we to do that now?"

The Pharaoh nodded. "Yes, I would like to show you around as soon as I can. We can even visit your father's Temple if we have the time," he added.

A smile instantly appeared on Aneksi's face. "That would be wonderful!"

"Then let's get ready," the Pharaoh said, extending his hand. Aneksi grasped it and stepped to his side.

As the two began making their way back inside to ready for the outing, the sound of a guard approaching fast stopped them. The Pharaoh turned to see one of the Palace guards kneel, head bowed. Aneksi peeked over her shoulder as the guard spoke.

"Your Greatness, may you exceed in this life and the one to come, have mercy for my intrusion. I bear a message from the physicians tending to your esteemed son, Prince Ankhetep."

Aneksi felt the Pharaoh's hold on her hand tighten. She looked his way, eyes softening with sympathy.

"Neferkempi." Aneksi blinked, waiting for him to go on. The Pharaoh did not look her way as he continued. "I want you to go inside and wait for me until I say otherwise." He let go of her hand. Aneksi bit her bottom lip and nodded, before walking away. The Pharaoh turned to watch her go. Although Aneksi gave no resistance to his order, he knew she would be upset for being told to back off so suddenly. But he could not bring her to Ankhetep; there were just some things she could not be seen involved with. And one of those things included his son's sudden sickness.

Once Aneksi disappeared behind the curtain of their chamber, he faced the guard.

"Speak."

The guard hesitated, looking up, and quickly brought his head back down.

"Your Greatness' presence is requested to confirm the results of the Prince's deteriorating condition."

"Deteriorating?" the Pharaoh repeated. The Palace guard stiffened.

"I...forgive my word choice, your Greatness. I did not mean to alarm you." The Pharaoh sighed and waved a hand at the Palace guard.

"Take me to them," he ordered. The guard nodded and jumped to his feet. "Where are they?"

"The physicians have gathered at the medicinal chambers."

"And the High Priests are still with them?"

"Yes, Your Highness. They are accompanied by four of the High Priests." The Pharaoh clasped his hands behind his back, straightening his shoulders. Four High Priests. That meant one was missing.

The medicinal chambers were split into six halls; one for where the ill were kept, another for material storage, another two for record-keeping, another to shelve herbs, animal tinctures and experimental treatments, another for surgical practices, and the last for preparing the dead. Along the walls were inked depictions of the lioness-headed woman, goddess of the knowledge within the halls. And among them were also blessings to the god Imhotep, the first and greatest physician, as well as architect and vizier to his King.

The Pharaoh knew his son would be placed among the latter of the chambers. A sudden, and very much serious, affliction like Ankhetep's would not be taken lightly. And if Ankhetep's condition had not improved since he last received news, there was a great chance the physicians could do nothing more and the Priests nothing but prepare a ritual for him on his journey to the Afterlife.

Reaching the entrance to the surgical hall, the Palace guard jumped ahead of the Pharaoh to move the curtain hung over the doorway. The Pharaoh ducked his head as he entered, and he halted to adjust his eyes from the bright light of Ra to the shadowy flames of Sekhmet. He clenched his jaw at the sight of the few bowed heads of the men before him, for Ankhetep still lay unconscious on a bed beside them.

The first to speak was Kiya's father, the High Priest of Isis. He stood tall and confident as the Pharaoh did, with only creases about his eyes that indicated his age.

"I will begin this, even if your bride's father isn't present," he said with a deep frown.

"This is not the time to bear your grudges, Isiskah," the Pharaoh replied in a dismissive tone. Isiskah wrinkled his nose but continued.

"We have discovered that your son -*my* grandson- was poisoned."

The Pharaoh narrowed his eyes, waiting for more.

"He tested positive for arsenic," one of the physicians clarified. Kiya's father sent him a glare and the man bowed his head in shame.

"But there is something else that is bothering the boy," came the voice of Kahorus. The Pharaoh turned to him. With thick arms and a larger belly to match, it was the High Priest of Horus, Ahset and Akhara's father, although the two were half-sisters. "Arsenic would not stop a child from waking up. Therefore, there is something else -that none of the physicians can detect- that is causing his unconsciousness."

"But he is not completely gone," Amenhath, the High Priest of Hathor, and father of Khemut, interrupted. Small in size and voice low, he was the kindest spirit among them, and his presence would have been looked over, had he not spoken. "Sometimes we heard the Prince Ankhetep call for you."

The Pharaoh felt his heart catch in his throat. He nodded at the priests for their insight and turned to the fourth who had remained silent: The High Priest of Sekhmet, Ekmati, grandfather to Meryt. Sekhmet was the goddess of war and fire, so Ekmati was the most notable in not just weaponry, but of medicine; he was also responsible for teaching every physician in the Palace what they knew.

The Pharaoh swallowed hard, anticipating what the elderly priest would say.

"What Kahoras is implying, and what these men are unwilling to admit openly, is that the young prince is being cursed by the gods." The Pharaoh made a strangled noise, in vain attempt to qualm the fear and shock of what Ekmati said. Such a statement could not be taken lightly. Ekmati continued, despite the Pharaoh's reaction. "It is clear to me; entombed in his body is a darkening soul. Only the gods could have brought this upon the son of a Pharaoh."

Blinking furiously, the Pharaoh rolled his shoulders, unable to remain still. If Ekmati had declared it a curse, then what he had seen earlier in the Nursery was no trick of the eyes.

"Can we do nothing to cleanse Ankhetep of it?" the Pharaoh asked, eyes searching the faces of the High Priests.

"Would it not be best to first identify which god or goddess inflicted this-?" started the High Priest of Hathor.

"Who has time for that?" growled Kahorus. "Right now, I say it's best we treat his physical illness first. What do you suggest we do, Ekmati?" The High Priest of Sekhmet's eyes narrowed the slightest, but he nodded.

"What is easily treatable should be our priority."

"Then that shall be our route," the Pharaoh agreed. But the stillness in the air spoke the truth of the situation.

To cease a god's wrath was impossible.

PART V.

Alone in their private chamber, Aneksi kicked off her leather sandals to lie down on the bed. She absently wondered why the Pharaoh would keep her away from anything regarding Prince Ankhetep. Finding no other reason than the fact that she wasn't the boy's mother, her thoughts trailed back to Lithra. Aneksi trusted the Pharaoh's words. Yes, something must have come in the way of their relationship. But what had caused it?

Aneksi turned her body to face the ceiling. Lithra's behavior had noticeably gone from its usual smiles to stern silence sometime after the Pharaoh publicly declared that he planned on marrying Aneksi.

She smiled at the thought, reimagining the moments they first met.

Minutes after Aneksi's father had told her the Pharaoh would be coming to visit her, she had snuck away to the Temple, hoping she could pray for Ra, Ma'at or Osiris to change either her father or the Pharaoh's mind about the marriage. Like the other daughters of the High Priests, she was locked into marrying the Pharaoh since birth. But unlike they, Aneksi was the only child of the Tri-God Temple's High Priest, the Lord-Priest Kairunamete. There was no other sister who could willingly take the position if she refused.

Aneksi had no interest in the affairs of the Palace or marrying the Pharaoh. Life at the Temple was devoid of any responsibility or care of what others thought, and it was sufficient for all her desires and comfort. Aneksi had even heard rumors circulating from the servants that the Pharaoh's relationship with each of his other wives was loveless and cold; he was marrying them as it was his duty to the High Priests, and her chastity was all he would want from her. Who would willingly accept a marriage to someone like that?

On her way there, with feet bare and hair set free from its usual braids, Aneksi had stumbled upon a stranger who had beaten her to the temple mount. He had turned to face her but Aneksi hid behind one of the columns that held up the outdoor temple. For a few minutes, they played the game of cat and mouse, Aneksi rushing from column to column to hide her identity, until the stranger stopped to laugh out loud.

Aneksi would never forget that sound. It was the sound that brought her hope for a fate of her own choosing.

Aneksi's smile grew into a grin, remembering how miserable she felt every time her father glorified her set marriage to the Pharaoh. And yet she had fallen in love with him without realizing it.

"Ani!"

Lithra poked her head into the open doorway, a scroll in hand. Aneksi pushed herself up, leaning on her elbow.

"Yes?"

"This is for you," she answered, walking to hand Aneksi the scroll. "I believe it is from His Excellency."

At this, Aneksi sat upright fully to take the outstretched letter. Not much time has passed since he had left- so when did he have the time to send for a scribe and write a letter to her? And for something so trivial? Too curious of its contents, she broke the Royal Seal and read:

My dearest bride,

I would like you to take your servant and leave for town. I will only keep you waiting. I have already addressed the driver where to take you and where to have you settled before I join you.

As always, your King,

Son of Amanrakh, grandson of Tyamun,

seventeenth King of the Nile, Bearer of the gods' Glory.

Aneksi frowned. She did not like the idea of leaving the Pharaoh and explore on her own. And the formality in his letter was unfamiliar to her. But she sighed lightly and laid the letter on the bed. The Pharaoh was worried about his son. How could she ask to take him away when Prince Ankhetep needed him the most?

She turned her head to face Lithra and gave her slave-friend a smile.

"How does riding into town as a Royal servant and friend to the Pharaoh's bride sound?" Aneksi asked. Lithra's eyebrows raised the slightest.

"You do not mean to go out on our own," she answered. "Neither of us have any knowledge of the outside." Aneksi forced a smile this time.

"Yes, it will be a bit strange," she conceded, "but the

Pharaoh expects us to go. I say we honor his request for the time being."

Lithra stood silent for a moment before nodding.

"Alright then. Let's have you dressed up for a public scene," she said, holding out a hand. Aneksi caught her breath at Lithra's act of friendship and took it with a beaming smile.

"Yes! Oh, and you should dress up as well, Lithra. I am sure they will have wonderful clothes for you to wear!" Lithra gave a tight-lipped smile.

"Of course, Ani."

At the medicinal chambers, the Pharaoh called for a scribe.

He was sitting in the sofa the servants had brought him, leaning into it as he massaged his temple. All the High Priests, other than Ekmati, left after their small conference. They had scheduled a mass ritual in two days if Ankhetep's health did not change.

The scribe arrived later than expected, but the Pharaoh did not put too much thought into it.

"Address this to Neferkempi's father, the Lord-Priest Kairunamete." The scribe bowed his head and began writing. As the Pharaoh spoke, he frowned to himself. "Tell him I am disappointed that he was not present when he was summoned. I would like for him to come to the Palace exactly after reading this message, wherever and whenever that may be, and he must never again delay his arrival when called by his King." The Pharaoh listened to the scratching of the pen with his eyes closed. Once it stopped, the Pharaoh opened his eyes. "Now, fetch yourself another scroll. I would like to send word to Neferkempi." The scribe looked up at the Pharaoh, his eyebrows furrowed in confusion. "Well? What are you waiting for, scribe? I have no time to waste." The scribe shook his head and retreated.

The Pharaoh leaned forward to sign the scroll, doing so in clean flourishes. He placed the quill meant only for him back onto the stone desk the scribe had brought. He also took the time to read over how the scribe had written the note and nodded his approval.

The scribe returned with a new sheet of papyrus, bowed, and took his place behind the stone desk with a frown. Now settling back into the sofa, the Pharaoh addressed his young bride. The Pharaoh settled back into the sofa.

"Write: My Neferkempi, I would like to remain with my son during what free time I do possess, and so we will not be leaving the Palace until he is free from this...illness. Do keep this letter as a reminder that I wish for your understanding in any times of trial that may separate us. Forever I am yours."

Aneksi did not recognize anything.

The dirty streets, the hunched people staring at their passing palanquin, the wandering furry creatures- neither did she recognize the driver or the Palace guards that led her out of the Palace through dusty, cobweb-filled corridors. She glanced over her shoulder to Lithra, who sat on the opposite side of the palanquin, dozing off. Aneksi gripped her arms, feeling a sudden chill pass through her.

When at last the palanquin came to a stop, Aneksi nearly cried out in happiness. The Palace guards stepped to the curtained doorway and used their forearms to create a stairwell for her to walk down. Aneksi gripped their shoulders and did her best not to strain the men longer than necessary. The Palace guards stood upright once she had stepped down, leaving Lithra to get off the palanquin on her own.

Once on the ground, Aneksi looked around at her surroundings. She caught sight of a large establishment before her. Despite the long ride and the decayed homes they had passed by to reach here, the place looked decent. Most of the stone was carved from sandstone and hints of imported obsidian, and there were tall, cracked pillars surrounding each side. Aneksi could only assume it was a pit-stop for any traveler of high status. But it did not look at all like it had seen visitors as of late.

"Shall we go in?" Lithra asked. Aneksi jumped at the sudden sound. Lithra grinned. "Do not tell me I frightened you, Ani! You would swim through the Nile after dark knowing crocodiles swim within it," she teased. Aneksi gave her a small smile.

"You only startled me. But yes, let's go in. I am quite hungry."

Lithra nodded and began walking towards the establishment.

"We can request the patroness of this inn to prepare us all a meal and a refreshment for you," she said.

Aneksi followed after her, looking back once at the empty horizon from which they had come. Her gaze traveled up to the blue, afternoon sky. The clouds parted once or twice to allow Ra's light to shine down upon her, but the chill in Aneksi's blood did not go away.

PART VI.

Aneksi sat on the thin bed the patroness had called "her

finest." The chamber was sparsely decorated with mismatching and holed curtains, terribly drawn and colored wall paintings of large birds, a dirty woven basket, and a rag in the corner of the chamber. And to make matters worse, Lithra had previously stepped out to relieve herself, leaving Aneksi by herself in the one-candlelit chamber. She could not fathom why the Pharaoh would want to spend time in such a low-end inn but thanked the patroness for the hospitality with a smile.

On her lap was an open herbal and substances book; Lithra had brought it over to read to pass her time but had lent it to her for the time being. However, Aneksi only skimmed the words and glanced at the drawings. Medicine did not interest her as much as it did Lithra. Her servant had always found it interesting how ordinary plants and consumable products could be used for various purposes.

The door creaked open.

Aneksi looked up at the sound, seeing a teenaged girl carrying a tray in her hands.

The girl trembled in her spot for a moment, causing the items on the tray to rattle. Aneksi made a move to get up and help her, but the girl shook her head of beaded, messy braids and took a step forward. And then another. And another until she reached the bedside.

From here, Aneksi could see that on the tray was a tall vase of wine, a full cup, a plate of bread, fruit, and a chipped jar of honey. Aneksi gave the girl a small smile.

"You seem so frightened and I apologize that I am the reason for your nervous behavior," Aneksi said. "I ask you to treat me as you would any other guest," she added.

The girl gave no response but furious blinking and a crease to her brow.

Aneksi gave in to her silence and let out a small sigh, thanking her before making a reach for the cup. As she did so, the girl let out a strangled yelp and threw the tray onto the floor. Aneksi froze in her position, her arm still outstretched.

The vase and cup shattered, spilling their dark contents on the faded, threadbare rug. The bread and plate had flipped over, and the fruits lay scattered. One rolled to hit the bottom edge of the bed.

The girl sank to the floor, holding her head, sobbing. Aneksi watched her, concerned.

"I'm so sorry," she mumbled, "My brother...I'm so sorry. For Ma'at.... I'm so sorry."

Aneksi held her breath, watching the girl shake and cry. Her eyes trailed to the spilled food and then to the open page in Lithra's book.

Poison.

Just at that moment, Lithra came running into the room. She skidded to a halt, chest heaving.

"Ani? What is going on?" Lithra shouted. "What happened here? Ani!"

Aneksi brought herself to look up at her slave, eyes watering. "I think she wanted to poison me," she whispered, curling her hands against her abdomen. "Oh gods, she was going to kill me."

Lithra's eyes widened and she rushed to where the girl's hugged herself, heaving uncontrollably. Lithra then grabbed the girl by the hair, forcing her to her feet. The girl cried out as Lithra yanked her away from the bed.

"How dare you attempt such a thing?" she hissed. "I will have you publicly executed for this!"

Aneksi gasped, a tear trickling down her dusted cheeks.

"Wait! She couldn't do it. She stopped herself, Lithra! I swear by Ma'at, she saved my life!" Lithra glowered at the girl in her grip, who remained limp in her hold.

"The law does not change for circumstances," Lithra shot back. "This girl will be dead for what she has attempted, and I can swear to you that is what will be done."

"Gods, no," Aneksi shook her head, holding a fist to her chest. "She was so sorry. Oh! Actually, she spoke of a brother. Perhaps he set her up for this. Or maybe she was forced by someone because they have her bro-"

"Enough!" Lithra shouted. Aneksi blinked at the fury in her voice and her commanding tone. Such behavior was punishable in a slave. Lithra took a deep breath, closing her eyes briefly before she spoke again. "Ani, your life is valuable. To have it come to such a close end is unfathomable and unforgivable."

"But Lithra-"

"No, we are done with this matter. We are leaving for the Palace with this criminal. She will no longer be a threat to your life, Ani."

Aneksi watched Lithra push the girl out of the chamber, calling for one of the Palace guards. She then closed her eyes and pressed herself against the cold wall, feeling sick to her stomach. Who would go as far as to want her dead? She could think of no one so desperate to act in the disfavor of the gods and commit murder. For some time Aneksi remained in that position, praying for the Pharaoh to come and take her away. And why had he even have her sent to such a dangerous place?

A half-hour had passed and Lithra had yet to return.

Aneksi forced herself to open her eyes. What was taking her so long? The chill in her body had gotten worse- to the point that her fingernails were turning blue and her teeth had begun to chatter. Something was not right about this place. Grabbing the herbal book, Aneksi stumbled out the door, tracing a hand along the walls for support.

"Lithra?" she called out.

There was no response. Just the chill in the air, and the whisper of the gods in her drumming ears. She heard a snap.

Aneksi turned around in time to see a shadow sneak by from one end of the hall to another. Swallowing hard, Aneksi made a bolt for the exit, once more calling out for Lithra. They needed to leave, now. Someone wanted them dead.

The sun was no longer high in the sky; instead, it had already begun its descent into the western horizon.

"Lithra! It is not safe here, we must-"

Aneksi ran straight into a solid figure and fell onto the ground with a yelp. She looked up to see the person she had run into, holding her stinging nose. The figure was hooded, and their bulging arms were wrapped in what appeared to be thick, coiled snakes. Aneksi shifted herself away from the looming figure, and kicked sand and sediments towards them, feeling her breath quicken.

"Who are you? And where is my servant? Why are you here?" Aneksi demanded, rising to her feet.

"Your slave no longer serves you and you will not be among us for much longer." The figure then raised an arm to retrieve something from his back.

Aneksi paled at the sight of a gleaming saber, its edge spattered with dried blood. The head of a falcon was etched in the saber's hilt and was staring coldly at her.

He made a full swing at her, but somehow, Aneksi's feet pulled her back just in time; time slowed just for those seconds for her to see the curve of the blade miss her chest by a mere fraction. The figure had swung again, but once Aneksi's feet touched the ground from her previous movement, she slipped, and crashed to the ground, dodging the second fatal blow.

The figure roared in frustration, turning around to face Aneksi's shaking form.

"Why will you not touch my blade?" he hissed. Aneksi breathed hard, picking herself up. She winced at the pain in her right ankle. The figure ignored her, staring ruefully at their outstretched arm where they gripped the falcon-headed hilt of their saber. "I always kill."

Aneksi took this chance to escape. She spotted something dark moving up the road and made a move in that direction, but as soon as she pressed her foot down, her ankle popped, and she plummeted to the ground once again. The figure grabbed her hair before she fell and let out a satisfied grunt. Aneksi shut her eyes, sparks of pain shooting up her scalp.

The figure poked the skin below her hairline with his saber, smiling widely, and said, "No more getaways."

"You let Her Grace go!"

Aneksi opened her eyes at the unfamiliar voice. Coming from the direction she had tried to run off to, were two men, running towards them. As they neared, they almost looked familiar. Had she seen these two men before?

"No. She will die!"

With one clean motion, the figure made a swipe to end her right then and there, but Aneksi twisted her head away from the figure's vice-like grip. The saber only caught her hair, ripping the two-feet dark curtain of braids clean from her head.

Tumbling away, Aneksi found herself falling in the outstretched arms of one of the two men. Aneksi clung to him, feeling the ever-evident cold breeze on her bare neck as the second man rushed to meet the hooded figure's oncoming saber with his own sword.

"Your Grace, my name is Rai. I will take you away from here. Merik will delay the assassin. You are safe now." Aneksi could barely hear his comforting words, nodding anyway. "Hold tight now," he advised, lifting her into his arms. "It will be a very difficult journey back to the Palace."

PART VII.

The noon sky was a bright, warm blue. But the Pharaoh felt a chill down his spine. He was on his way back from visiting the two men he had fired that morning. They had accepted their former Palace uniform, thanking the Pharaoh for being so compassionate towards them after they had erred in their duties. The Pharaoh had smiled and told them it was because of his considerate new wife they were able to continue working in the Palace once again.

When the chariot came to a stop, the Pharaoh stepped down and called for their midday meal to be set.

On his way to meet Neferkempi, a servant interrupted the Pharaoh. His personal guards, as usual, surrounded him, obscuring his view of the servant speaking. The Pharaoh frowned at the disruption but allowed them to speak. Relaxing his shoulders, he leaned against the hallway wall with closed eyes, excited to tell Neferkempi about his recent doings.

"Your Highness forgive me for my incompetence, but her Grace is nowhere to be found," the servant whispered.

The Pharaoh opened his eyes, his head whipping in the servant's direction as he pushed himself off the wall. He shoved away his personal guards to stare down at the bowing youth.

"What did you just say?"

The servant shuddered in her spot.

"Her Grace...Lady Aneksi...we could not find her. She did not receive your-"

"Then find her you wretch!" the Pharaoh shouted, towering over her. He had lost a hold of his anger and his breath came out in hard, fearful gasps. How could Neferkmepi be gone? Where could she have gone? With whom? And how could this happen on their first day married?

The girl made a guttural noise, nodding her head, and cowered as the Pharaoh stormed past, heading straight for where he left Neferkempi last.

The Pharaoh's mind raced at the thought of something ill-fated happening to her. Kidnapped? Beaten? Murdered? Ransomed?

He tore through the curtained entrance to his private chamber. The bedsheets lay wrinkled, but there was no one inside the chamber. His rising anger was fueled more so by fear as the Pharaoh threw open doors, plowed through any tailor's chamber he could find, and barreled through the consort chambers in vain search for his beloved.

When he came up short, the Pharaoh marched his way through the Palace, calling for his viziers. They rushed to his side, speaking all at once with ideas on how to find his wife. The Pharaoh let their chatter sink around him as he sat slumped in his throne, defeated. How could she have just vanished? His eyes then caught sight of his two reinstated personal guards. Seeing them, the Pharaoh sat up.

"Come forward, you two," he said. The viziers hushed as the two men looked at each other before walking toward the Pharaoh. "Neferkempi showed her mercy to you. It is time you return her favor."

Aneksi heard shouts. They were followed by the sound of spears clanking and the thundering voices that included calls for execution.

"Please, let his Greatness judge me for what I have done!"

Aneksi blinked open her eyes. That voice. She knew who

it belonged to. She looked across from where she lay to see Rai with his arms tied around his back, and the Palace robe he had been wearing ripped off his back. Several other Palace guards held him at spear-point.

Merik and Lithra were nowhere in sight.

Pushing herself up, Aneksi frowned. Rai had rescued her from the people who tried to kill her. Why were they treating him like this?

"Neferkempi?"

Aneksi froze at the sound of the Pharaoh's voice. She slowly turned her head to face him, where he stood at the doorway of the chamber. Her eyes watered at the worried expression on his face.

The Pharaoh rushed to her side, kneeling on the ground before the bed. Instinctively, he reached over to run his hand through her hair but Aneksi winced, turning her face away. She could not bear to have him see her the way she was.

"Dear gods," the Pharaoh whispered. "What did they do to you?"

Aneksi took a shaky breath and forced her eyes open to stare at the Pharaoh. Her heart beat, angry and loud in her ears.

"But you did this to me," she accused. The Pharaoh

reeled back, as if she had slapped him. Aneksi pressed her hands together, swallowing back the bile in her throat. "You told them to take me there. You tried to poison me!" she cried, the tears now spilling down her cheeks. "And then you sent an assassin to make sure I was dead! And all this–" Aneksi's voice cracked, but she forged on, "–all this after our very first night together. Oh gods, they were right," Aneksi pushed herself away from the edge of the bed, pulling up her knees to her chest. She rocked back and forth, tears blotting out her vision. "Oh gods, they were right," she repeated.

"Oh, my Neferkempi." The Pharaoh inched forward, slowly easing himself onto the bed. The Pharaoh then turned his head to the Palace guards and Rai. "Leave us," he ordered, "and do not allow for any disturbances."

The guards grunted in acknowledgment and began to leave. Aneksi looked up at the commotion and blinked the tears out of her eyes in time to see Rai being escorted out of the chamber.

"No!" she cried out, lurching forward.

The Pharaoh caught her by the shoulders with his arm. "Neferkempi–"

"Rai saved me from the assassin! Him and Merik!" Aneksi gasped, turning to the Pharaoh. "Where is Merik? And Lithra!

Where are they? Are they dead? Gods, don't tell me they are dead like I should have been!" The Pharaoh motioned for the men to go and they did. Rai did not look back. "Tell me!" Aneksi gripped the Pharaoh's bicep, her wide eyes staring right at him.

The Pharaoh cringed inwardly, seeing Aneksi in such a delirious state. Whoever was responsible for this, he vowed, would be punished greatly.

"The guard, Rai, will return to search for those you seek to see again," he assured her.

"But they are treating him like a criminal!" she cried. The Pharaoh brought a hand to wipe away her tears, his fingers barely grazing her cheek.

"His mission to rescue you was kept a secret. Someone in this Palace must have been involved in your kidnapping and I could not risk anyone else knowing what my plans were for finding you. The Palace guards were simply doing their duty. He will not be harmed I can promise you." Aneksi let out a sigh of relief. "But tell me, you said I told you to leave the Palace? How and when did you receive this message? And from whom did you receive it?" When Aneksi remained silent, the Pharaoh clenched his jaw. She didn't trust him. "Neferkempi," he said in earnest, "I swear on this beating heart of mine, I did not wish any of this upon you. In fact, I had sent you a letter stating the opposite."

Aneksi's shoulders slumped; she could not bring herself to resist the urge to trust him. Aneksi closed her eyes briefly to remember everything as it had happened.

"Lithra came to me not long after we parted ways this morning. I did find it odd you were able to have it sent to me so soon, but I left anyway." The Pharaoh raised an eyebrow. "It had the Royal seal, and your signature," Aneksi added. "Why would I have thought to question its origin?"

A slow smile made its way to the Pharaoh's face. She would never have thought to doubt any letter that claimed to be from him, with or without a royal seal. After all, before he had revealed himself as the Pharaoh, every piece of correspondence sent to her was never linked back to the Palace or signed by any name. It was in her nature to be so trusting of others.

Aneksi blinked in confusion at his smile, her inner emotions swirling in a pool of anger, regret, and curiosity.

The Pharaoh slipped his arms around her waist, bringing her body to his.

"Will you ever forgive me for allowing this to happen to you?" he whispered. Aneksi shut her eyes, curling against the

Pharaoh.

"Just find Lithra," she whispered back. "And Merik."

The Pharaoh kissed the side of her head.

"I promise I will do all that I can."

They stayed like this until the candle wax melted, dimming the light in the chamber. Aneksi dozed off and fell asleep, but the Pharaoh remained awake throughout the night. He could not bring himself to close his eyes or let her go; for every minute he had spent the night holding her reminded him of every minute of the day he had spent worrying for her return.

It was not till dawn when the Pharaoh gently laid her down onto the bed. Ekmati and his granddaughter, Meryt entered then, stepping lightly to not disturb the two. Ekmati set himself to open the wooden windows of the medicine chamber to allow Ra's light in. Meryt set down a jug of water and plates of food by the bed-stand should either of the two wake up hungry.

The Pharaoh did not notice their arrival, too focused on Aneksi's sleeping face. He lifted his hand to run it through her short, uneven hair. Closing his eyes, he finally succumbed to sleep.

Meryt tiptoed over to the bed and pulled the bedsheet

over them. Though he was her husband and father of her daughter, Meryt felt no hate in her heart for seeing the two. After all, the gods had chosen this life for her.

"Sleep well," she whispered.

Turning away, she hurried after her grandfather, knowing Aneksi's arrival would mean there was much they would face in the coming days.

PART VIII.

The Pharaoh opened his eyes, stretching his arms above his head with a yawn. Where Aneksi should have been was an empty bedside. The Pharaoh nearly jumped as he scrambled to get up and find her, fear welling up in his chest. At the sound of the door opening, the Pharaoh quickly turned around. He let out a sigh of relief at the sight of Aneksi walking in. She stopped short, seeing the Pharaoh awake and staring at her.

"Come here, Neferkempi," he said, motioning for her to return to the bed. Aneksi did as he said, slipping under the sheets with him. But she kept her gaze downcast, refusing to meet his eye. The Pharaoh wrapped his arms around her, resting his chin on her head. "Tell me what's upsetting you," he said, stroking his thumb back and forth against her thigh.

Aneksi gripped the edge of the bedsheet as she spoke.

"They told me they found Merik and Lithra," she said, gazing out the open window. The Pharaoh held his breath, fearing what she was going to say next. "Lithra is hurt, very badly, and-" Aneksi stopped herself, feeling tears well up in the corner of her eyes, "-and Merik, they found him dead, cut to bits-"

"Shhhh," the Pharaoh stopped her, but she had already begun to shake, sobbing. He rocked her, holding her close.

"They came in harm's way because of me," Aneksi said through her tears, "because of me Merik is gone and Lithra is dying!"

"No, don't think like that," the Pharaoh countered, giving her a squeeze. "Your life is precious, Neferkempi. They served you well." Aneksi sniffed.

"Are their lives not precious, as well?" she asked, turning to face the Pharaoh. He gave her a small smile, leaning down to kiss her nose. She closed her eyes briefly, her cheeks heating up at the tenderness of his kiss.

"Yes, their lives are precious. And that is why they would give it up for yours. It proves how much you mean to them as their Lady."

Aneksi buried her head in the Pharaoh's chest, shutting

her eyes. She had never thought of herself that way- to be worth the lives of all those who served her. The Pharaoh sighed, wrapping his arms around her, and pressed his lips to her head. He reached a hand to run his fingers through her ear-length hair and felt her tense. But the Pharaoh smiled to himself.

She was still his Neferkempi, his beautiful storm, no matter what.

Breakfast was eaten in bed. Bowls of water were brought to the Pharaoh to wash himself and tables were arranged to accommodate them to move as little as possible. Ekmati supervised the food and drinks being brought in with a solemn face. The Pharaoh made eye contact with the High Priest of Sekhmet and nodded in gratitude.

Aneksi fidgeted were she sat, her eyes furiously moving from one plate to another, her heartbeat racing. She was starving but suppressed the urge to eat all at once. She looked into the eyes of the servants who entered and monitored their hand positions, judging their intentions towards her. Had she met them before at some point in her life? Were they relatives of anyone she had come across? Had she treated them fairly? Was this why her mother taught her to treat servants with kindness?

The gentle back and forth strokes of the Pharaoh's thumb on her thigh broke Aneksi from her frantic thoughts.

She felt him lean towards her and whisper, "I confess to you; I am the Pharaoh and you are a temple's servant, but by the gods, I will make you my bride."

Aneksi's eyes widened. Those were the exact words the Pharaoh had said to her nearly a week ago when he revealed his true identity to her. When he had confessed that he loved her for the first time.

The words made her think back to their initial meeting and how they had been able to enjoy each other's company without the pressure of their titles preceding their notions of one another.

"Step forward and tell me your name," he had said after laughing, *"so I may ask of you to the Lord-Priest."*

Aneksi froze, clutching the edges of the column she was hiding behind. If her father had found out that she had escaped from her nursemaids' clutches and was hiding out at the temple when she was to be readying for the Pharaoh's visit, he would be ashamed of her. No, she could not tell this man who she was.

After a moment, she walked out of the column's protection. Keeping her gaze low, she said, "I am only a servant of this Temple.

Call me as you will."

The man's face fell.

"Ah, a servant." Aneksi could feel the sound of his disappointment in her heart. He glanced down at her uncovered feet, then to her wild hair, and finally settled to her face. "Then I call you Neferkempi." She bowed her head, accepting the name.

When Aneksi looked up, the man had turned and already walked down the steps. She stared after him, feeling her heart beat ever so quickly beneath her breast.

Who was he? His rich-colored robes and gold jewelry marked him a wealthy man. But to see her father personally was almost impossible by even the richest of merchants. Just before he disappeared from view, the man turned back to look at Aneksi. She felt her heart skip a beat under his sudden gaze. That man. Was he the answer to her prayers?

But just like that, he was gone.

There was a shuffle behind her. Aneksi turned to see Lithra, settling down on the temple floor.

"What are you doing out here?" she asked, tilting her head in question. "I brushed the tiles and wiped the columns down already. You do not need to do it." Aneksi sat down beside her.

"I am here because I don't want to marry the Pharaoh," she said.

"So, what am I to do? Aren't you to meet with him now?"

Aneksi thought a moment. "Lithra, I need you to go in my stead."

Lithra jumped to her feet, wide-eyed.

"If anyone were to find out, I will be executed!" she cried.

"Please," Aneksi begged, holding her servant's hands. "You have a fair face. He'll never suspect you to be a servant, especially once you bathe and wear my clothes. Plus," she added, "If you act with no interest, he will not return. You know well that the Pharaoh is happy with his last wife and their infant son, may he live to reign a thousand years."

Lithra stomped her foot in frustration. "Only if you tell me why you do not want to marry the Pharaoh."

Aneksi hesitated, but relented, saying, "I think the gods have shown me another."

"Better than the Pharaoh?" When Aneksi said nothing, Lithra shook her head but smiled at Aneksi. "For you, Ani, and your tremendous courage, I will." Aneksi stood up to embrace her servant-friend. Lithra laughed and hugged her back. "But if the Pharaoh continues to visit, what do you want me to do?" Lithra asked after Aneksi had let go. Her face had lost all its previous warmth. "Knowing your father, he will make sure you marry the Pharaoh at any cost."

Aneksi looked towards the three marble statues at the center of the Temple. Ma'at, the Truth. Ra, the Light. Osiris, the King.

"We shall take it as it comes," she answered.

Aneksi blinked the memory away. She smiled, knowing he was distracting her from her worries. She turned to face the Pharaoh, and said, "But allow me to confess O Pharaoh; I am the true daughter of the Priest and the one you thought her is my servant. Would you marry me still?"

He smiled back at her and answered her the same way he did then.

"You could be anyone, Neferkempi, and I would love you as long as the Nile still runs."

PART IX.

Meryt adjusted the headdress Aneksi was to wear on her official visit to town with the Pharaoh while a servant unwrapped the bandages from her right ankle.

A week had since passed from Aneksi's last outing.

Meryt's daughter, Thut, also sat on a stool nearby, playing with a doll on her lap. Now that her foot had healed, the Pharaoh had suggested they go out as retaliation to whoever had wished her dead; she was alive and well, unhindered in

61

her role in the Palace with the Pharaoh at her side.

"Does it fit you to your liking now?" Meryt asked, moving away to allow Aneksi to look into the mirror a servant was holding up for her.

Aneksi turned her head to see her profile. She could see the front of her hair, pushed up and held in place by the crown, while the veil that had been sewed onto the edges of the headdress hid the rest of her neck. No one could know that her hair had been cut or link it to the rumors that had been going around. It would be unfavorable if the public knew too much of the incident.

"Yes, it does, thank you."

Aneksi gave Meryt a small smile and nodded at the servant holding the mirror to lay it back down. Aneksi's clasped hands tightened a bit, at the thought of Lithra. She turned to Meryt, who stood beside her.

"Am I allowed to visit my slave before I go?"

"The injured one?" Meryt tucked a strand of her dark hair behind her ear. "I am afraid not."

"Oh," Aneski sighed. She then stood up, dwarfing Meryt, who was nearly six inches shorter than she. "Then I shall be off." Meryt nodded and opened the door to the chamber to let the guards know Aneksi was ready to go.

One of the two guards was Rai. He had been given a finer uniform to wear, personally requested by the Pharaoh. Instead of the regular leather over their cream-colored sleeveless tunic, Rai wore a gilded bronze chest-plate padded at the shoulders that exposed his torso, and a knee-high shendyt, or cotton kilt, held in place with a thin, leather belt.

Aneksi smiled at him, glad to see him. He made no other response other than a half-bow, but Aneksi did not mind, turning away with a smile still on her face. She was simply glad he would serve to protect her from now on. As she made her way to the Palace gate, Aneksi caught sight of Kiya walking through the same hall as she with her attendants.

Aneksi stopped to stand aside, her head slightly inclined and her gaze on the floor. Kiya was, after all, higher in status for being a consort to the Pharaoh longer than Aneksi. From the corner of her eye, Aneski saw Rai place his free hand over his side, where a dagger was clipped to his belt.

Kiya made no acknowledgment of Aneksi's presence. She indicated with her hand for her slaves to keep up with her strides.

"Do you not smell this foul odor? Quickly before it lingers on my skin," she said, wrinkling her nose in disgust.

Aneksi stood there, rigid at the insult until Kiya had

turned the corner. She closed her eyes momentarily before continuing her way. She exited the Palace to see the Pharaoh already waiting, and surrounded by his guards, and quickened her pace. The Pharaoh saw her approaching and, smiling widely, offered his hand to help her onto the chariot.

With a firm lift, Aneksi swayed in the one-man chariot, grabbing onto the front rail to balance herself. The chariot was U-shaped and was painted white and gold with markings of Ra along its sides. Leading it were four glowing white stallions, harnessed together by wooden splints pressed against the flanks of the horses on the outer sides.

Aneksi furrowed her eyebrows. How could she ride and drive the chariot on her own? This was not what she expected when the Pharaoh had told her they would be sightseeing the town together. Just then, Aneksi felt someone step onto the chariot behind her. She felt her heart lurch to her throat as the Pharaoh adjusted his footing, pressing against her body.

"Did you think I'd have you steer a chariot when you've never done so before?" he asked, briefly placing a hand on her waist. Aneksi pressed her head against the Pharaoh's shoulder, her eyes closed, and her lips curled in a smile.

"I'm ashamed to admit I was a little worried," she replied, opening her eyes and turning her head up to look at the

Pharaoh. "But I'm grateful that I'm wrong."

He laughed and kissed her forehead, a mischevious gleam in his eyes. "It's just like you to think that way, Neferkempi."

The Pharaoh then turned to the guards that surrounded them, on foot and on the backs of mud-colored horses and signaled with his hand for them to be off. Aneksi turned to face forward, and with the Pharaoh at her back, they rushed to meet the crowds.

As they rode into town, men and women peeked from their homes to catch a glimpse of the new bride. Some threw flowers and petals at Aneksi and the Pharaoh, and some youths ran at the heels of the horses with sticks to imitate the Palace guards.

Aneksi also noticed girls, adorned in their finest cloth and jewelry, sat upon wooden seats shouldered by their men-folk in hopes to catch the Pharaoh's eye. Aneksi kept her face passive, but she grimaced internally at their blatant effort at seduction. A week had only gone by since her marriage and yet they thought it appropriate to do this. The Pharaoh did not pay any mind to any of them, preoccupied with showing Aneksi all the town's marketplaces, temples, and routes that led to nearby farmlands and villages.

When at last they reached the farthest edge of town, the

Pharaoh pulled the horses to a stop. The horses snorted and flipped their tails while one of the guards dismounted to treat them.

Aneksi turned around to watch the Pharaoh step off the chariot with a small jump. She swallowed hard when he turned to face her. A misplaced jump would likely bruise her. The Pharaoh smiled at her unease and then quickly crossed his arms over his chest with a frown, feigning an upset look.

"Neferkempi, does this small hurdle stop you from being at my side?" he accused, turning his back to her.

Aneksi tilted her head, contemplating on how to respond to his invitation to play. She glanced at the guards, seeing that they had fanned out, and then leapt from where she stood. Aneksi collided into the Pharaoh's back and nearly knocked him off his feet. She heard something tear but did not take heed of it.

"No, it does not!" she answered, wrapping her arms around his neck. The Pharaoh grinned and hefted her properly onto his back.

"And where would my Neferkempi like to spend the rest of the day?"

Aneksi looked up at the afternoon sky before resting her head on the Pharaoh's shoulder.

"Take me anywhere," she said, closing her eyes.

There had been a kernel of fear in her stomach throughout the entire chariot ride, expecting her public appearance would once again make her a target to the assailant who tried to kill her. But nothing had happened. Whoever wished her dead had separated her from the Pharaoh; therefore, she assumed they did not want the Pharaoh to be involved.

The two were heading to the nearest building. The guards had already cleared the rooms and investigated the owners before they even reached it.

The Pharaoh collapsed to his knees at its entrance. Aneksi stepped off the Pharaoh's back and turned to face him. The Pharaoh gave her a weak smile, doing his best to hide his exhaustion and heaving chest. But she knelt down anyway, worried.

"Had I known I would take so much out of you, I wouldn't have made you carry me here," she said, wiping away sweat from his brow. The Pharaoh caught her hand.

"If it means that you would not soil your feet or make your breathing heavy, I would gladly do it again, Neferkempi." Aneksi shook her head but smiled and helped the Pharaoh to stand up again.

The building was more a home than an inn. It had a single chamber for lounging, an even smaller sleeping chamber, and two cellars. In the back was a yard with an open fire pit and grinding floor for bread and beer. And unlike the Palace and temples, it was made of clay bricks, not stone.

Aneksi looked around the living chamber, admiring how small the shelved statutes of the gods and goddesses were along the walls. The Pharaoh headed to the smaller chamber, settling onto the sleeping mat, still recuperating. Aneksi followed after him and, with not much other furniture for her to sit on; she sat down on his lap.

A few moments later, several male peasants entered carrying bowls of water, a wooden low table, and plates. Aneksi felt her heart skip a beat at the thought of eating in an unknown place, but felt the Pharaoh press his arm around her waist as a reassurance. She saw Rai standing at the doorway, watching over the servants as well.

The meal consisted of duck eggs, cooked quail, and two bowls of *molokhia*, a soup made with molokhia leaves, garlic and diced duck meat. There was also a small bowl of fruits and honey, along with a plate of bread. For drink, there were large vases filled with freshly pressed wine.

It was clear the food had been sampled beforehand as

protocol; a few slices of bread from the center and edges were gone, an indent in the honey and *molokhia* indicated someone had taken a spoonful of it, half a duck egg was missing, and small bits of the quail were also eaten.

Aneksi made move to get off the Pharaoh's lap so he could eat, but he pulled her back down.

"Stay," he urged, using his left arm to hold her waist. "Let's eat together." Aneksi nodded with a smile and set herself to wash her hands in the water bowl.

Without the formalities of being around the royal court, the Pharaoh relaxed.

He teased Aneksi openly about the birthmark she had between her shoulder blades, saying it looked like a bird's wings and laughed loudly when she countered that the dark spots on his neck from the heat were no better. He talked with food in his mouth and gave her sloppy kisses when she turned her back for more food. Aneksi could not remember a time she and the Pharaoh had let their walls down and simply enjoyed each other's company so frivolously since the first day they met.

When the leftovers and utensils had been taken away, the Pharaoh leaned against the wall of the chamber and stretched out his legs. Aneksi sat in front of him, between his legs, and the two sat there, content.

But in the silence, Aneksi's mind quickly wandered back to the falcon-wielding assassin. Did living as royalty mean accepting and living with the risks of assassination?

"If the gods allowed you to be anyone else, would you remain being the Pharaoh?" Aneksi blurted aloud. The Pharaoh exhaled, and his shoulders slackened in momentary thought.

"Perhaps a merchant," he finally said. "There is dignity in doing such work, and as one, I will have the ability to command and have leisure still."

"So you would choose to be a lesser Pharaoh," Aneksi said, looking his way. He smiled.

"Yes, exactly so." The Pharaoh then added, "And what would you choose, Neferkempi? If not the daughter of the Lord-Priest." Aneksi held his gaze.

"Another merchant," she replied, "So that we may come across one another in our travels and fall in love again." And also, because Aneksi could not think of a reason one would ever have to kill a merchant.

The Pharaoh wrapped his arms around her and kissed the base of her neck in response to her words. Aneksi smiled, but the smile did not last. Did the Pharaoh not worry about his safety? Aneksi closed her eyes and tilted her head as he continued upwards, slowly making his way to her lips. But when he reached there, he paused, his eyes lingering on Aneksi's face. There were no windows in the chamber, and the only light came from the candles in the next chamber.

But even with her face half immersed in shadow, the Pharaoh could tell Aneksi's eyebrows were knitted and she was frowning slightly as if she were holding back some pain.

"Aneksi," he said. She opened her eyes immediately, eyes wide and lips parted in shock.

The Pharaoh had never called her by her birth name and it worried her now that he did.

"Neferkempi," Aneksi corrected, "to you I am Neferkempi." The Pharaoh sighed.

"You're upset about something, Neferkempi, yet haven't disclosed it to me," he told her.

Aneksi stared into his dark amber eyes and looked away. She knew if she spoke her mind she would only trouble him more than he needed to be.

The Pharaoh, seeing that Aneksi was staying obstinate in the matter, leaned forward and kissed the space behind her ear. It was her weakness. Aneksi let out a small moan when he kissed her again.

"Neferkempi, tell me," he breathed against her skin.

Aneksi sighed.

"I'm still overwhelmed by what happened to me," she said, keeping her gaze low. "The poison...the assassin...How can I make your worry all over again about it when all you have done was try to ease it away?"

The Pharaoh frowned, and creases formed above his brow. He clenched his fists. How could he call himself her husband when she was tormented so?

"So, my efforts have been in vain."

"I- no-" Aneksi fumbled, alarmed that she had upset the Pharaoh. He should not be when he was doing his best.

"No, Neferkempi, you may smooth over my other faults, but not this one." Aneksi's eyes watered at his sharp tone of voice. She hated seeing the Pharaoh upset. Especially if it was over something she was involved in. "What am I doing wrong, Neferkempi? How do I make your fear go away? How can I keep you happy like I used to?"

Aneksi grabbed the Pharaoh's face in her hands and crashed her lips to his, her eyes shut tightly. For a second, the Pharaoh was absolutely still, shocked that she had made the first move. When they parted seconds later, Aneksi pressed her forehead to his, breathing heavily.

"Please let me overcome my fears on my own. I want only what is best for us both," she whispered to his mouth. "And right now, what's best is to forget our worries exist."

From outside the doorway, Rai walked over and blew out the candles that lit the house. Going back to his post, he leaned against the wall, and with a hand on his hip, he closed his eyes.

The night would be awake tonight.

PART X.

Aneksi woke up with a start. She placed a hand on her forehead, feeling it to be damp with sweat. She propped herself up on her elbows looking up and breathed hard at the sight of the new surroundings. Aneksi blinked a few times, remembering that she and the Pharaoh had spent the night out, not at the Palace. With a sigh, Aneksi fell back onto the mat, turning to settle in the crook of the Pharaoh's arm when she bolted upright, realizing he was not at her side.

Ra's light shined in from somewhere, illuminating the chamber as if it were daytime. Aneksi pressed the bed sheet to her body, her heart beginning to race. There were no windows in the chamber, how could it be so bright?

A shadow fell across the doorway, followed by a sickening

thud of something falling to the ground next to her. Aneksi mouth went dry and she turned around. Her breathing faltered at the sight before her. Rai lay motionless in front of her, his eyes open and blood trickling from the edge of his mouth.

"Oh, gods no," Aneksi whispered, a hand over her mouth.

The assassin had come for her.

A wind blew in from the doorway, stirring Aneksi's hair. Aneksi furrowed her eyebrows and grasped the long strands of silken ebony with a racing heart. Hadn't her hair been cut by the falcon-sabered rogue? Was she dreaming?

Crunching sounds startled Aneksi out of her thoughts. The floor was somehow now littered with bones of all sizes, some stark white and others a decaying yellow. And as wide as the doorway stood her assassin, his gleaming weapon dripping with fresh blood. Aneksi trembled and her throat constricted.

"You die today," he growled, stepping over Rai's lifeless body.

"Have you no restraint?" Aneksi said, forcing her voice to remain steady. If this were a dream, she would wake up from it. "Your Afterlife will surely be miserable for the atrocities you commit!"

The man said nothing, but the snakes around his arms hissed and continued to coil along his biceps.

Aneksi felt her determination waver the closer he came. There was nowhere she could escape to nor was anyone here to rescue her. She pressed the sheet to her body, fear welling deep in her chest.

"I have done nothing to you!" Aneksi finally cried out, tearing up. The man stood before her, his arm rose to finish her.

"What you have done is as impersonal to me as what I will do to you. I am only a deliverer, and I deliver the news of your death."

Aneksi covered her face with her hands and shut her eyes. It was over. The dream would end now.

The man struck his blade down and she winced. But he had sunk the blade into the skeleton-filled ground instead with a crunch. Aneksi held her breath before looking up at the man. He was grinning; his leather-like skin crinkled deeply around his mouth and beady black eyes. And just as suddenly, he whipped the saber out of the ground and slit her throat clean.

"-Be gone!"

Aneksi's eyes snapped open to see her father bent over

her, his eyes narrowed in concentration. He wore a tall, white and gold embroidered head-piece and a flowing robe to match. Aneksi blinked repeatedly, sitting up.

"Father?"

Kairunemete leaned back into the chair beside her bed with a loud sigh.

"Your hair," he was the first thing he said, frowning deeply. "What happened to it?" Aneksi bit her lip, and her gaze strayed to look around instead of answering her father.

She was back in her designated consort chamber, and none but she and her father were present. It also looked to be morning since the doorway curtain was tied up to let the light in. The Pharaoh must have returned to the Palace with her while she was still asleep.

Aneksi looked back at her father, playing with a strand of her short hair, and mumbled, "It was cut."

"By whom?" he demanded. When Aneksi said nothing, her father slapped his knee in agitation. "Aneksi, speak." She shut her eyes briefly before answering.

"I do not know! But he wanted me dead, Father." Kairunamete sighed at the desperation in her voice.

"Of course, they would," he replied, leaning into the back of his chair, "you are the gods' blessed daughter wedded to the Pharaoh. Your future is brighter than anyone else's." Aneksi frowned. It did not reassure her that her father expected such evil crimes to happen to her. "Describe the man to me." Aneksi curled her toes under the blanket over her, feeling uncomfortable.

"He was tall," she started in a low voice. "And had a darker complexion...and I think he had snakes on his arms."

"Mmm," Kairunamete's lips curved down the slightest and he closed his eyes. "I see. Tell me about his weapon. That is what he used to cut your hair, no?" Aneksi nodded.

"A bird's head," she said, tilting her head to remember, "was on his sword." Kairunamete's eyes opened.

"A bird?" he repeated. "What kind?"

"I...I cannot remember for sure."

"Recall it, Aneksi."

"A falcon?" Aneksi suggested.

Kairunamete's face darkened.

"And he has your hair," he said in a harsh whisper. Aneksi cocked her head.

"I suppose. They were not able to recover it. Oh!" Aneksi's eyes widened. "Have you heard of Lithra's condition?"

"Your slave girl? Yes. A pity." But it was clear her father

was still brooding over the fact that the man who wanted her dead had a falcon on his sword. Kairunamete then fished for something in the pocket of his robe, retrieving a thin chain that contained a small pyramid of solid gold. There was a symbol engraved on it. Aneksi bowed her head for her father to clasp it around her neck. "Wear this at all times. The gods will cease the nightmares. However, if you do have another after today, send for me immediately. He has your hair; whoever he works for can still find other ways to disturb you."

When she lifted her head back up, she clenched her hands into fists.

"Why do they do this? What do they have to gain at my harm?" Kairunamete wrinkled his nose.

"Evil exists, Aneksi. And when evil exists, those who are blessed suffer from their sorcery."

"Sorcery?" Aneksi echoed.

Kairunamete nodded.

"Yes. The kind of torment you just tasted is the mark of sorcery. Your hair is what they are using to tie you to their little spells. That must be the reason why your hair was not found. Whoever is doing this knows exactly what they are doing." Aneksi frowned, fear churning her stomach. With just her hair they could torture her without even laying a finger on her? "Aneksi," her father said, placing a hand on her head. "Don't keep your thoughts on this matter. Your father is here, and he will not let any of their magic harm you anymore."

She smiled at the determination in his voice. Her father was the strongest priest in all of the Blacklands, second to the Pharaoh. There was nothing she had to worry about.

Aneksi gave Kairunamete a small smile and asked, "When did you come by the Palace?"

Kairunamete waved the question away with his hand.

"I was told to do so the other day when Ankhetep fell ill. I was at your mother's shrine by the Nile, so my arrival was tardy."

"Oh."

"There will be a ceremony for the boy," her father said, changing the subject, as he stood up from his chair. "So, keep praying. There is hope for him."

Aneksi smiled. "Of course."

Once he had gone, some servants arrived to help Aneksi dress. Meryt arrived just as they stepped away, and invited Aneksi to bathe at the spring with the other wives of the Pharaoh.

Aneksi lightly brushed her fingers on Meryt's hand.

"Meryt you are kind to me. But I cannot guarantee the others will react in the same manner. And for that reason, I do not wish to be so close with them." Meryt let out a small laugh, catching Aneksi by surprise.

"They will all feel contempt for you in these early days. It is only natural for them to be jealous."

"Then may I ask why you have not shown at for me as Lady Kiya has?" Aneksi blurted. Meryt nodded thoughtfully, her expression sobering.

"I have lived in these halls since birth. Marrying the Pharaoh changed little for me. Lady Kiya had to fight for her place in the Palace."

"Were you against wedding the Pharaoh?" Aneksi asked, eyebrows raised.

"You could say that. I wasn't madly in love at the time of our marriage, but neither was I spiteful." Aneksi nodded. "It was more of a convenience for my grandfather. When I reached of age, he thought marrying the Pharaoh was a fitting way for me to find my permanent place here."

"But since the High Priest of Sekhmet works here, shouldn't there have been a place in the Palace secured for you already?" Aneksi asked.

"Not quite. My father was against me remaining in the

Palace. He knew of my interest in medicine and thought it could go to better use at our Temple in Memphis for some reason or other. I also have three younger sisters in Memphis, who could have easily married the Pharaoh in my stead. But I personally did not like my father's plan, as it meant I would leave the Palace for good; neither did my grandfather. So, instead, he had it that I would marry the Pharaoh in order to continue my medicinal studies here, under his supervision."

Aneksi nodded again. "Ah, I see. I risked quite a lot when I thought to go against my father. I am glad it ended well for the both of us." Meryt smiled in understanding. Aneksi spoke up again saying, "Truly, I am grateful for your kindness. Princess Thut will certainly grow to be a wise young girl."

"If only she weren't so steadfast in doing everything I tell her not to do, I would believe you," Meryt laughed, holding a hand out for Aneksi to take. Aneksi gratefully took her hand and allowed Meryt to lead her out.

"I did not know it was so hard to raise a child," Aneksi said.

"It is only so difficult because I am active in Thut's upbringing. I have seen how the other princesses love and view their wetnurses as mothers, and I would not be comfortable with Thut having that bond with any other woman but me." Meryt stopped walking. Aneksi looked away from her to see that before them was a screened archway. "Here we are."

When Meryt pushed aside the curtains, Aneksi's eyes widened at the sight before her. A large square pool -the size of her consort chamber- lay before her, filled with steaming water. The bottom had been painted over in a teal blue paint, giving the water a hazy blue tone. Surrounded by it were cushions and potted palm trees. A canopy of see-through mesh cloth hung over the entire place, allowing Ra's light to shine down on the water, but not enough to heat it.

"The servants will be here with the soapstone and flowers," Aneksi heard Meryt say as she strode over to the edge of the pool. Aneksi remained where she stood while Meryt took off her sandals and began to unhook her dress. "Just as long as you do not do anything to upset the other wives, I think you will have a relaxing time here before we are called for breakfast," Meryt added over her shoulder.

PART XI.

It was indeed difficult for Aneksi to remain on the good side of the Pharaoh's other wives. Aneksi did her best to be silent, fearing if she spoke, she might say something to offend the other. But her presence alone seemed to conflict with them.

Ahset and Akhara walked in together and stared at the newcomer in their midst. Aneksi bowed her head at them, feeling her cheeks flush at the assessing look they were giving her. The two then turned away and allowed their servants to unclothe them before stepping into the water. They stayed in their respective corner of the pool, glancing over their shoulder at Aneksi as they whispered.

It was the first time Aneksi got a clear look at them; the two looked almost identical, and quite like their father Kahorus, the High Priest of Horus, with round faces, olive bulb noses, short black hair, sun-baked skin and a body type that leaned toward large rather than slim. Aneksi would not call them ugly, but the more you looked at them, the less pleasant they appeared. And their constant scowling look did not help.

Meryt, seeing Aneksi's unease, swam towards her to place a comforting hand on her shoulder.

"Do not stress yourself over them," she said with a smile. "Ahset and Akhara, being the first to marry the Pharaoh, have always been a little angrier than the rest of us."

Aneksi nodded, but she frowned anyway. Of course, she understood; if the Pharaoh had taken a liking to someone after their marriage, Aneksi knew she would not be so keen to be the new bride's friend. She should not assume that they felt any different for her.

Khemut arrived a few minutes later. Aneksi did not even know she had entered the spring until a servant walked over to her to begin messaging oils into her hair. Khemut looked Aneksi's way once or twice but said nothing. And her looks were not as malicious like the ones Pharaoh's first two wives had given. Khemut was perhaps the youngest of all the first five wives, and Aneksi guessed she must have been in her early teens when she married the Pharaoh. Aneksi tried to smile in her direction but received only an expressionless stare in return.

The final wife to come was Kiya, and her entrance was not so easily missed. Two servants held the curtains for her to enter through and another three servants held skincare herbs, folded towels, and a tray of scented soaps and oils behind her. Khemut swam to the other side of the pool, settling between Meryt and the Pharaoh's first two wives, to allow Kiya a side of the spring all to herself.

Meryt did not have as much trouble fitting in with the wives as Aneksi did. She watched as the petite woman was able to have small conversations with all the present wives-even Kiya nodded in her direction with a look that did not bode any ill intent. Aneksi held her arms against her chest, pressing as far away as she could from everyone and none minded her presence nor appreciated it.

After several more minutes of this, Aneksi placed her hands on the stone ledge of the pool and pushed herself out of the spring. Her vision blurred with unshed tears. She did not want to spend another second in a place where she was not welcome. The other wives had every right not to like her, but that did not mean she had to endure it when she did not need to.

Aneksi made a grab for the folded towel set for her when a black scorpion, the size of her thumb, dashed out from it. Aneksi shrieked and slipped as she tried to get away from it, falling back into the pool. The other wives quickly retreated to safety, shouting at the servants to capture and kill the venomous insect.

When Aneksi regained her senses and swam back to the surface to breath, she was alone. The wives had deserted the spring and had taken their servants with them. Even Meryt was gone. It was as if they had never been there.

An eerie silence followed after. Aneksi wiped her eyes and slowly swam back to the opposite side of the pool.

"Rai?" Aneksi called out, her heartbeat remaining at a fluttering pace. "Rai!"

Relief flooded through her veins at the sight of her personal guard rush to the sound of her call. He had a hand over his eyes as he approached, stopping a few paces away.

"What happened?" he asked, turning his head left and right to pinpoint her location. "I heard screams but did not see you leave." Aneksi blushed furiously at the state of her need and was grateful Rai was covering his eyes.

"There was a scorpion in my towel," she confessed. Rai's eyebrows lifted in surprise. "And the servants have all fled."

Rai, now knowing where Aneksi was, turned his back and sat down, lowering his hand. He placed his spear down; his shoulders were taut, and he gripped his knees as he spoke.

"Are there no clothes here for you to wear?" he asked, his head fidgeting from having to force it to stay still.

Aneksi looked over her shoulder. Her previous clothes had been taken away for cleaning when she had first entered the pool. The only towel that remained was the one that had harbored the scorpion. And Aneksi was not at all willing to go near the towel again.

"No," she said in a low voice.

"Then I shall fetch a slave–" Rai started.

"No!" Aneksi felt her face burn hotter at her own command. "I don't want to be alone. The scorpion could still be here," she added, looking away. He hesitated, understanding the awkwardness of their circumstances, and then began to unclasp the chest plate he wore. "Rai–?"

"Wear it," he said, turning slightly to hand it to her, "so I may go look for the scorpion." Aneksi nodded and reached out to take it. It smelled a little musky and the metal was heavy, but she pulled it over her head anyway.

After fumbling with the strap, it locked in place. Aneksi glanced up and said, "You may turn around."

Rai stood up and Aneksi held her breath. Her lower half was still bare; though the water was dark enough to obscure her body if Rai accidentally looked that way. While her breast was covered neatly, everything from the bottom of her ribcage to her bellybutton was still visible above the water.

Fortunately, Rai did not look her way as he hunted for the scorpion that had caused all of this. Aneksi watched him chase after it behind a potted plant before spearing it with his weapon. Aneksi forced herself to look away when she caught herself watching the muscles in his shoulders and back glisten when the clouds parted to let in Ra's light.

Aneksi felt her heart calm down and, feeling braver at the

sight of the dead scorpion, headed over to the towel on the ledge of the pool.

"This is where it was hiding," she told Rai. He nodded mutely and walked forward to examine it for safety.

The towel was clean and new, and the small jar that had contained the scorpion fell out from inside the folds when Rai lifted the towel. It shattered and Aneksi winced as bits bounced into the water.

"Gods forgive me, are you hurt?" Rai nearly shouted, stooping to one knee to push the fragments of the glass jar away from the water's edge. "I should have been more careful- I am so sorry your highness! Forgive me!" Aneksi shook her head.

"No, it's alright." She paused before adding, "Is it safe to wear it now?"

"Oh, this? Yes." Rai looked away as he handed the towel to Aneksi. She blushed and quickly used it to tie around her hips.

When she was done, she asked, "You do not mind if I make your uniform wet, do you?"

Rai titled his head, looking briefly back at her.

"No-"

Aneksi held her breath and dove below the surface of the

pool. She opened her eyes and began her search for the fallen glass pieces. No one but she and Rai knew of it being in the water, and she did not want anyone to step on it unknowingly and hurt themselves. Once she retrieved as much as she could in one go, Aneksi resurfaced to place them with the other glass shards of the jar.

Rai had moved away and was speaking with two servants, one of whom was holding a change of clothes in their hands. Rai turned to see Aneksi and directed the servants to her before taking his post outside. The two servants undressed her, patted her dry, frisked and combed her hair, oiled her skin, and fit her into a loose cotton robe and gave her minimal jewelry to wear.

Aneksi nodded her thanks and stepped out of the curtains with Rai's armor in her hands.

"Thank you," she said, unable to meet his gaze. Rai nodded and took the chest-plate from her.

Aneksi hesitated before walking on to where the other wives would be waiting to have breakfast with the Pharaoh. She hoped the news of the scorpion did not reach him. Perhaps this incident was a punishment for their outing yesterday? If that were the case, the more the Pharaoh worried and doted over her over these harassments, the more the culprit would become angrier. After all, both this and the nightmare had come the morning after they had spent the day out in public.

For now, her only option was to relieve her worries to her father and stay away from the Pharaoh until something could be done about the situation.

PART XII.

The wives of the Pharaoh were shocked, to say the least, when Kiya was called to sit by the Pharaoh's side that morning. They all glanced at one another before finally looking at Aneksi. Despite what anyone in the dining hall could assume it meant about her relationship with the Pharoah, Aneksi was relieved that she was not at his side. She worried that he would question her anxiousness and she did not want him to know about what had happened earlier that morning.

Kiya, however, basked in the Pharaoh's favor. After everyone had entered, and when Aneksi taking her original place at the table, she walked in; each of Kiya's steps were calculated and slow, and her hips swayed with every step in the revealing dress she wore. The light fabric was cut low in the front, and the sides neatly clipped to accentuate her breast and expose the sides of her flawless, waxed legs. The Pharaoh took her hand and guided Kiya to his side, smiling a little. He remembered that he had loved her for her pride and beauty. She would need to maintain this strong demeanor for tonight's ritual.

But having her so close again also reminded him of what had torn their relationship apart. He let go of her hand as soon as she was situated and turned away. It was her need to be perfect, for perfection in all aspects of her life. It gave little room for the Pharaoh to be anything other than a pharaoh, no matter where he was or who was watching.

The Master of Servants praised the Pharaoh and his predecessors, and the meal commenced. Aneksi could not help but pick at her food and stare at the table; her stomach was twisting at the thought of everything that had happened to her in the past week or so. Why was it that everything and everyone seemed like a threat or possible suspect to her?

When breakfast was taken away, Aneksi rushed out of the dining hall. Rai followed after her. Although he said nothing, Aneksi knew he was forming conclusions about her actions. But she did not confide in him about it, not wanting him to be any more involved than he already was as her guard.

Aneksi made her way over to the garden behind their private chamber and sat down at the foot of the Ma'at statue.

She gripped the edges of the statue's base, pressing her forehead against the marble with her eyes closed. Aneksi did not know how to deal with what had been happening to her since coming to the Palace.

Was everyone at the Palace an enemy of hers? Who could she put her trust in?

Aneksi felt the gold chain her father gave her sway in the warm breeze. She knew her father was very protective of her, but the charm would only ward off the nightmares. Who was to say she could not be kidnapped again and be taken back to the assassin with the falcon-sword? Was there even a way she could put a stop to it all?

The sound of someone approaching her back broke Aneksi's thoughts. She waited to catch the pattern of their gait and smiled faintly to herself upon recognizing it. The Pharoah walked with a slight drag in his right heel, thus making the sound of his left sandal hitting against the ground different than his right's. His right step made more of a grating sound before he lifted it up to continue walking. The Pharaoh had blamed it on a bad knee.

Aneski made a move to stand up to acknowledge his presence but felt the Pharaoh's hands on her shoulders to have her remain crouched. He stood behind her and she could feel his knees brushing against her arms.

"I want to believe you left on your own because you were jealous that I called my First Wife to sit with me and not you." Aneksi held her breath, waiting for him to continue. "But I knew you were preoccupied about what happened this morning at the bathing pool."

Aneksi's eyes snapped open and she turned around, wide-eyed. She slowly stood up, maintaining her gaze with the Pharaoh.

"How...how did you find out?"

"Did you think I would not know when my Neferkempi goes to bathe without me?" the Pharaoh asked, cocking his head to the right with a smile. Aneksi pouted, unable to reason with the amusement the Pharaoh found in the situation. Seeing her reaction, the Pharaoh cleared his throat. There was no point in trying to lighten the situation. "I'll admit I was careless, Neferkmepi, when it came to your wellbeing within the Palace walls. I didn't think anyone would want to harm you so desperately. The others may not admire one another but they have lived side by side for all these years without much problems. I only expected the same treatment for you." The Pharaoh reached to caress her cheek with his thumb, his eyes softening.

"Please do not worry so much for me," Aneksi said, lowering her gaze. "I did not marry you for that. I only wished for us to be happy, but these past days-" she cut herself off a moment before continuing on, "-these past days my happiness has become shrouded in fear. I can't overcome it."

The Pharaoh briefly closed his eyes and shook his head at her words.

"Neferkempi I do not want you to fear for anything, do you understand? This is not the life I envisioned for us nor do I wish to tolerate it." The Pharaoh's voice was stern, and they made Aneksi look up at him. "After I learned about what happened this morning, I made several accommodations to ensure your safety every moment of the day," he continued, "and I have spoken with your father as well. He assured me he made arrangements of his own for your protection. So, for now, you have nothing to fear."

Aneksi exhaled, feeling her chest was somehow more hollow, freer, hearing those words.

"Thank you," she whispered.

The Pharaoh smiled. "Now come with me," he said, running his hand down from her cheek to her shoulder. Aneksi felt her cheeks begin to heat up at the look in his eyes. "I would like for you to overcome this morning's incident by spending some time with me."

Rai had his eyes closed as he leaned against the wall that led to the bathing spring. On the other side of the spring was one of the Pharaoh's many personal guards; Rai did not know him as an individual, but only knew that the guard came from one of many families who served to protect the royal family for generations.

He opened his eyes to see a Palace slave approach. Rai straightened up and peered down at the girl.

"The High Priest of Sekhmet seeks an audience with His Greatness regarding the Prince, may they live healthy lives for a thousand years."

Rai did not recognize her as a servant of the medicinal chambers but also knew that the Pharaoh had switched all roles among the servants and guards since hearing about Aneksi's scorpion encounter. He not only switched their positions but their timing shifts as well. Guards who manned the stables during the day were stationed in the kitchens for a night shift while the previous guards were sent to oversee the front gates during the evening; servants who laundered in the morning were sent to the medicinal chambers during the evening, and those former servants were then be sent to wash the floors and maintain the gardens during the day. The rotations would happen at any given time as the Pharaoh saw fit until someone was found guilty of aiding in Aneksi's kidnapping and executed.

Rai nodded, and the girl turned back to where she had come from. He pressed a hand over his face and shook his head before resuming his original position against the wall. The High Priest of Sekhmet would have to wait until the Pharaoh was free to visit.

After some time, the curtains drew back and Aneksi and the Pharaoh appeared. The two were much more at ease than when they had first entered, their shoulders relaxed, and their movements were light and careless.

The Pharaoh had stopped to lift Aneksi's chin and closed the distance between them. The younger servants walking out of the spring, holding trays of bathing accessories, were blushing whereas the older servants were trying not to look and smile in the couple's direction. When the two had pulled away, Rai drew the Pharaoh's attention.

News of Prince Ankhetep's condition always dampened the Pharaoh's mood, but this time he only nodded and, with a small smile, told Aneksi he was going to visit his son.

Aneksi's eyes lit up and she quickly asked, "You usually

don't wish to have me go with you when you visit the Prince, but may I accompany you this time? I would like to visit Lithra. I haven't seen her since they admitted her into the surgical hall."

The Pharaoh hesitated a moment, before nodding.

"Of course."

Aneksi was anxious as she walked with the Pharaoh. He glanced her way and gave her a smile. She beamed at his encouragement and he laughed at the quick shift in her mood.

Once the two approached the medicinal hall, they split ways. Aneksi entered the chamber set for the ill, while the Pharaoh continued down the corridor to the chamber set for preparing the dead, which lay at the very end.

"If your slave happens to be conscious, let her know I share some concern for her health as you do," the Pharaoh said, halting before the chamber doorway. Aneksi nodded.

She was told that Lithra was asleep.

Aneksi's eyes watered to see her old friend wrapped in blood-stained bandages across her body. Aneksi was given a seat by the bed and she sat down to take Lithra's hand.

"Has she woken up since coming here?" Aneksi asked the servant who adjusted the bedsheets and aligned the rows of tinctures by Lithra's bed.

"Just here and there, Your Grace. Nothing longer than a few minutes."

Aneksi nodded at her and turned back to face her slave. Lithra lay motionless except for the rise and fall of her chest. She looked to be in some sort of pain: her eyebrows were furrowed, and she was frowning. Aneksi sighed and leaned forward with her elbows on the bed.

"Do you remember the time we first met?" Aneksi whispered, staring at their joined hands. "When my father brought you home, I thought you to be a living goddess for having such pale skin and beautiful copper hair. You were unlike anything I ever knew." Aneksi laughed a little at the memory. "I served you food and brushed your hair. And when you went to sleep I prayed that you would stay at my side as long as I lived. I even remember Mother telling me to treat you with kind words and actions because you suffered travels I could never comprehend." A tear rolled down her cheek and she swallowed back the emotion in her throat. "I might not have married the Pharaoh if I knew you would be in this much pain because of it."

Aneksi's hands were gripping Lithra's; she pressed it against her forehead, and her eyes were shut despite the stream of tears flowing from them.

"I wish I hadn't left you in that horrible place; I should have told Rai and Merik I lost you. I regret leaving you there on your own to this fate. Will you ever forgive me?"

A shadow fell over Aneksi and she felt a small hand on her shoulder.

"We need to redress her bandages," Meryt said in a low voice. "For your sake, I would prefer you to not be present when we do." Aneksi nodded and slowly laid Lithra's hand back to her side. "Thank you for understanding."

Aneksi took the offered handkerchief from Meryt and took a few steps to wipe away her tears and recover. She did not look back to see the single tear that had run down Lithra's cheek.

Two servants -one carrying a woven basket of freshly washed linen and the other an empty one- arrived, followed closely by a physician. They bowed in Aneksi's direction and turned away to treat Lithra. After Aneksi composed herself, she was guided back to Meryt's consort chamber where Meryt instructed wine be brought to them. Meryt's daughter, Thut, was there, lying on the floor with several different types of leaves in front of her.

"I don't think I have properly introduced you to my

daughter," Meryt said with a small smile as they waited for the servant to return. Aneksi looked over at the six-year-old kicking her feet in the air as she stared attentively at the plants. "Thut, come greet Lady Aneksi," Meryt said.

The girl turned over, and upon seeing Aneksi watching her, quickly stood up and ran to her mother's side. Her eyes were cast to the ground and she bowed her head. She had her mother's deep skin tone, but her facial features -her eyes, her nose, her lips, and her face shape- all belonged to the Pharaoh.

"It is an honor to meet you, Lady Aneksi."

Meryt smiled down at her daughter, clearly proud of her obedience this time.

Aneksi managed to smile, saying, "And what were you doing over there with those leaves?"

The girl looked up at Aneksi.

"I am studying them. I must be able to recognize every type of flower and plant given only their stems, leaves, or roots." Aneksi raised her eyebrows at the intensity of the requirement but Meryt's smile only grew wider. It was clear that Ekmati's family line would continue to remain in the boundaries of Imhotep's knowledge.

"Thut, why not show Lady Aneksi how much you know

already," she suggested.

Aneksi nodded in encouragement and the girl happily ran over to do as they asked.

While Aneksi spent time with them both, she could not help but feel some sort of envy that Meryt had birthed a child to the Pharaoh, who looked just like him. But she realized it was a petty feeling, for Thut had not chosen her father nor had Meryt her husband. Just as they were handed their lives to them, Aneksi would have to learn to make peace with whatever her life with the Pharaoh gave her, including his other wives and their children.

PART XIII.

During the evening, Aneksi was put into one of the guest chambers with the rest of the Royal Family. Their personal servants were put in another chamber, both under lock and key until the ritual was over.

Ahset and Akhara were settled in a far corner of the chamber, separate from everyone else. Their two daughters, Nebta and Hemetre, also stood by them. Here, Aneksi could clearly tell neither of the two girls looked anything like the Pharaoh; they were clear replicas of their mothers. Khemut sat by Meryt; and their daughters, Freyi and Thut, were seated at their feet, playing together with dolls. The dolls' bodies were made of wood and carved with blessings of fertility. The hair was made from horse tails or straw and the dress from various fabrics. Every girl, whether living in the Upper or Lower lands, either had or was acquainted with them.

Thut stood up and walk over to Nebta and Hemetre, offering them a doll as an invitation to join them. Akhara's daughter, Hemetre, being the tallest of all four girls, looked down her nose and smacked the toy out of Thut's hand in response.

Aneksi's only reaction to this was pure, silent shock. She gaped, seeing the doll's head roll away from its body. Thut picked up her broken doll and went back to Freyi where they resumed play as if the doll was still intact. Neither Meryt nor Akhara said anything. Khemut turned her head away, perhaps acting as if she had not seen the altercation. And by the silence of it, this must not have been the first time it occurred.

Aneksi swallowed hard when Akhara glanced her way, as if challenging what she had seen and if she would do anything about it. Bowing her head, Aneksi stared at the red rug beneath her feet, her hands clamped on the edges of her cushioned stool. Her eyes pricked with tears, feeling ashamed she could not stand up for Meryt's daughter nor ease the hostility that was being nurtured among the half-sisters.

It pained her more when Aneksi realized that should she have any children, she would be subjecting them to this same hierarchy.

May the gods help her.

At nightfall, the five High Priests, Kiya, and the Pharaoh all took their positions in the Palace's Temple chamber. The air was cool outside, but inside it was stifling.

Although Kairunamete was Lord-Priest, as his temple was an homage to three gods and not one like the other High Priests, he would not lead the ritual tonight. Every ritual and ceremony conducted at the Palace was led by the Pharaoh; he was known, after all, as High Priest of all Temples. Mounted on the front wall were eight statue busts of the gods -Horus, Sekhmet, Hathor, Isis, Ma'at, Ra, and Osiris- surrounded by two sconces on either sides of the wall and a single floor brazier beneath each of them.

The Temple chamber had no windows and the walls were painted black and marked with depictions of Seth, god of all chaos and disorder, but also an ally to Ra. The only light came from the wall sconces and the single fire. Shadows danced from every corner of the chamber, and the flames popping and crackling in the silence.

Prince Ankhetep had been moved from the medicinal hall to the center of this chamber, lying unconscious on the bed brought from the Nursery. Above him was a strand of rope that would open the ceiling door. The Pharaoh stood in front of the five High Priests, who had positioned themselves in an arch formation around the bed. Behind them were Kiya and a row of Temple servants.

Prior to this, the High Priests, the Pharaoh, Kiya, and the servants had cleansed themselves in the ablution spring; it was a large trench dug outside the Temple chamber filled with purified water and natron solution. Each High Priest had one for their respective Temple and no one was allowed to bathe or touch its water for any other purpose but purification for rituals.

The Pharaoh began by praising the gods. As he spoke, the High Priests recited hymns below their breath, in accordance with him. The Pharaoh lifted Anekhetep and walked before the statues, dropping to his knees before the busts and holding the young boy out to them. He gazed up at the stone, feeling the heat from the brazier make him break out in a sweat.

"I praise You in body and spirit, as one who will join You

in your existence in the sky. I beg You to remove the demon that plagues Your son, Our Ankhetep."

Kiya walked over to the Pharaoh's left, holding a vase of water from the ablution spring. She then slowly poured the water on Anekhetep's head, using her other hand to stop the fallen water from entering his nose or mouth. Some fell onto the metal brazier, hissing and turning into steam, and the rest splattered onto the stone.

Her hands shook slightly, and for a moment, Kiya doubted herself and imagined the vase slipping out of her hand and ruining the ritual. When the water had all been used up, Kiya wiped her son's damp hair and stepped away.

The servants took their position, each laying down on the altar by the fire the best the Pharaoh could offer: solid gold, spun silk, polished emeralds, pearls, wood, ripe fruit, golden raisin bread, wine, salted venison made from antelopes and waterfowl.

Everyone but the Pharaoh was to exit after this.

Before leaving, Ekmati ordered the servants to put out the two wall sconces, leaving the floor brazier at the altar to be the only source of light. He then closed the door silently shut and followed the rest of the attendees back to their own chambers.

The Temple considerably darkened, but the Pharaoh

waited a moment or two for his eyes to adjust. His arms ached from having hold Ankhetep for so long, but he clenched his jaws and endured it. He once more gazed up at the eight animal busts, whose eyes glittered down at him in the flame light.

"My son is pure and will grow to be Your faithful king if You allow it. I beg You," the Pharaoh said. His eyes blurred with tears, but none fell as he glanced down at Ankhetep's sleeping face and brought the boy to his chest. "I beg You, let not such a child be devoured by a restless spirit before he can show You his love."

The Pharaoh drew back and before he could stand up, he caught sight of the same serpentine shadow he saw at the Nursery appear along Ankhetep's face. The Pharaoh froze, watching it writhe below Ankhetep's skin before it slithered out from his ear. It continued to glide past the brazier and made its way to the bust of Horus and disappearing into the shadows of the chamber.

"Father?" The Pharaoh snapped his attention to the conscious child in his arms, blinking furiously. "It's too dark to see your face properly," Ankhetep said. "Have you been crying?"

The Pharaoh stared at his son for a second before

embracing him once more. He felt his son lean into him and the Pharaoh's tears finally came down.

Part XIV.

When morning came, Aneksi felt the coldness of the bedsheets, knowing the Pharaoh was not at her side. She opened her eyes and let her heart sink.

She lay there, remembering what had happened last night. After everyone had been released from seclusion, Rai had come to her and relayed a message from the Pharaoh: he would delay his retirement of the night for he wished to spend a little more time with Ankhetep but would return soon. Aneksi was too grateful to be among the few to know Ankhetep was feeling better so soon after the ritual that she did not think too much about what the Pharaoh said.

With a sigh, Aneksi sat upright and called for a servant. As she was being dressed, Aneksi glanced at the bed, seeing that only on her side were the sheets wrinkled with use. Contrary to what he had said, the Pharaoh had not come back at all.

Aneksi headed to the medicinal chambers to check up on Lithra, knowing breakfast did not start until the Pharaoh wanted it. And since she had not been told to do so, she could only assume he was still asleep somewhere or woken up early to play with Ankhetep.

Lithra was awake when Aneksi came by. Seeing her sitting upright, Aneksi rushed to her side, beaming.

"Oh, Lithra!" she cried, throwing her arms around her slave. "It is such a joy to see you!" Lithra said nothing and Aneksi pulled back, holding her at arm's length still smiling. "How do you feel?" Lithra smiled a little and shook her head.

"I ache all over," Lithra said. "That is all."

"Oh." Aneksi withdrew her hands before clapping them together. Lithra raised her eyebrow. "I did not tell you yesterday when I visited you as you were asleep," Aneksi began, "but the Pharaoh wanted you to know he wished you well for your recovery. You must be thirsty! Allow me to get you something," Aneksi continued, turning away to call a servant before she could see Lithra's face go red. "Bring Lithra a cup of wine, please! Yes, and something to eat as well." Aneksi turned back to Lithra, smiling. "I do not know what has come over me," Aneksi said with a laugh. "I feel like I have not spoken to you for years!" Lithra pursed her lips in an effort to smile but did not share so openly in Aneksi's revelry.

When breakfast time had come, Aneksi asked that she sit out, wanting to spend more time with Lithra.

Rai frowned at her request, seeing it as a counter to the Pharaoh's words from last night, but followed up on it regardless. He returned saying the Pharaoh had answered in the affirmative and Aneksi happily spent the rest of the morning with Lithra.

"Ani, what's that around your neck?" Lithra asked after they had eaten. Aneksi placed her right hand over the necklace her father had given her.

"It's just something Father gave me for my troubled sleep," she answered. Lithra's eyes narrowed Aneksi hesitated. She did not want Lithra to feel that she could be in danger as well and so changed the subject. "Lithra, I trust you very deeply, you know this," Aneksi began. Lithra nodded slowly. "So, will you accept a secret for me?"

"Of course, Ani." The two leaned closer to speak in a whisper.

"Prince Ankhetep is feeling much better after the purification ritual last night." Lithra's eyes widened.

"So soon?" she asked, then added, "How many know of this?"

"Just the Pharaoh, Lady Kiya, and now, the two of us."

Lithra leaned back, wincing a bit, but she nodded in Aneksi's direction. "That's a secret, indeed."

"It is! We mustn't repeat it. The Pharaoh wishes to be sure of the Prince's recovery before he announces it. I have no issue speaking of it to you; after all, you would normally have been present when I received the news." Lithra nodded before looking away.

"I feel quite strained, Ani. I would like to rest now."

"Oh, of course!" Aneksi nodded and stood up. "I will also get the physician and servants to redress the bandages as well. I will visit again if you call me, otherwise I shall return only tomorrow."

Lithra did not look her way. "Yes. Thank you."

Aneksi left the surgical hall in a bright mood, almost forgetting she was in a Palace living amongst those who disliked her. With Lithra and the Prince in recovery, surely, both her and the Pharaoh's worries were sure to be over. There was a skip in her step and Rai was assured it was because she had seen to her old friend.

Aneksi was heading back to the private chamber when a young boy ran right into her legs.

"Oh, gods are you okay?" Aneksi asked, bending down to gently touch his bald head. He looked up at her with wide eyes and Aneksi froze in recognition of the boy.

"Ankhetep, my Crown Son! What did I tell you about

leaving-!" Kiya stopped mid-sentence the moment she saw Aneksi. Her eyes narrowed, and she stomped forward to wrench Ankhetep from her.

"Ouch! Mother!" the boy cried out, shaking himself out of Kiya's grip.

"We do not associate with those beneath us," Kiya said, glaring at Aneksi.

"Beneath us? But she is beautiful," Ankhetep countered.

"What did you say?" Kiya blinked in confusion. Aneksi smiled at the young Prince, slightly bowing her head to him in acceptance of the compliment.

"The gods wouldn't bestow beauty to someone who wasn't deserving of it," the boy explained, turning to his mother. "That's what Father told me." Kiya pursed her lips and held her head high.

"Your father, the Great Pharaoh, is correct, but as your mother," Kiya said, emphasizing the words, 'father' and 'mother', "you must always listen to me, so you may learn how to see through this false beauty."

Ankhetep turned back to stare wistfully at Aneksi. She gazed back at him, amazed by his lack of resemblance to either of his parents.

"If she is false beauty then as Crown Prince, I shall turn

her to true beauty. I can do that, right?"

Rai turned his head, coughing into his fist, as Kiya's face went red with both anger and embarrassment at her son's words. Aneksi knelt and the boy leaned forward in anticipation to what she had to say.

"I–"

"That is enough, Ankhetep, you must see the physician now," Kiya cut her off, grabbing Ankhetep's hand and swiftly walking away. "I told you time and again you are not to be seen in these halls until you are fully recovered."

"But, Mother!"

Aneksi watched the Prince look back at her before being forced to keep walking forward. She slowly stood to her normal height and glanced at Rai.

She tilted her head, and with a smile said, "He has his father's charm."

PART XV.

"I expect a prince from you."

Aneksi looked away from her father, biting her bottom lip. It was evening and Kairunamete was on his way back to the Tri-God Temple and had come to say a few parting words to his daughter. The other three High Priests -Kahorus,

Isiskah, Amenhath- had already left the following morning. Ekmati stayed at the Palace, as he had a son, Meryt's father, already in his place at the Temple of Sekhmet.

"Prince Ankhetep already shows signs of a wise leader," Aneksi mumbled.

Kairunamete frowned.

"That is no excuse for you not to promise a better son." Aneksi looked up at her father and opened her mouth to speak, but her father waved a hand for her to stop. "Then think about it this way, Aneksi: any son you have would be able to stabilize the royal line if another illness befell the Prince."

"But I do not want him in any danger," Aneksi argued. "He is a good boy and he is loved dearly by his father."

"That is not to say your sons will be loved any less." Aneksi folded her arms over her chest and looked away. "Aneksi the Tri-God temple has placed more pharaohs on the throne than any other of the Temples. This last century we have been declining. I need you to honor our patrons, Aneksi, as I cannot." Aneksi remained silent, still refusing to look at her father. Kairunamete cleared his throat. "I shall be going now. Take care of yourself."

"Yes, Father."

She heard him walk out of the chamber without another word.

Aneksi turned her head back, only to see the door shut close. She shook her head and stood up, knowing her father was right.

According to their history, five centuries ago, the Pharaoh Akenamun had suddenly passed before he named a crown son. He and his Great Royal Wife had six sons, all of whom were a perfect fit for the throne. After many nights of constant quarreling, the Great Royal Wife chose the youngest prince, Akenanum, to take the crown. Despite their anger, the other princes loved their mother deeply and obeyed her decision. For their goodwill, and to further curb them from stealing the throne from their brother, the Great Royal Wife issued the construction of five Temples, naming each remaining son a High Priest of the patron god or goddess their supporters prayed to the most.

The five older princes agreed to their new position, contracting with their youngest brother that only consorts from their Temple lineage could be named Great Royal Wife. Ever since then, the five Temples -the Temple of Isis, the Temple of Horus, the Temple of Hathor, the Temple of Sekhmet, and the Tri-God Temple- had been competing to

114

place sons and consorts to the throne in honor of their founding prince. And because the eldest brother, named the Lord-Priest Amete, had been the closest to Akenanum, the Tri-God Temple secured more sons to the pharaoh's throne and more daughters with the title of Great Royal Wife than any other Temple.

Aneksi knew her father's keen desire for her to marry the Pharaoh had come from this, just as the other of the High Priests had done the same for their daughters. She had been raised to think this way, and Aneksi could not deny that she wanted to honor the founding High Priest of her temple, as well. But it felt wrong, knowing that Ankhetep's future would be in jeopardy if she were to have a son who could de-crown him.

Aneksi glanced down at her stomach, praying she would give birth to another daughter for the Pharaoh.

During the evening meal, Aneksi was once more seated beside the Pharaoh. The Pharaoh's eyes never strayed far from the hyper little boy who was once again eating with his family. Kiya did not hesitate to take the opportunity to now always be dressed in her finest, for she knew wherever she was, Ankhetep would be, and wherever the Prince was, the

Pharaoh was sure to check-in.

Aneksi, was no doubt, aware of this, but she did not want to nor could she compete with Kiya; the older consort was an ageless, ebony beauty.

But it all came to a peaceful lull by nightfall. The two lay in bed, Aneksi leaning into the Pharaoh's bare chest with the Pharaoh's arm around her waist. A slight breeze lifted the curtained doorway to the private garden, but the moon was too thin to shine down that night; instead, two candles burned by the chamber doorway, bright enough to shed light inside but also far enough to not disturb sleep.

Aneksi ran her forefinger along his chest, absently drawing swirls and curves along the Pharaoh's skin. He was speaking about Ankhetep, about the boy's birth.

"My father, before he went to the gods, told me to cherish my firstborn son and the woman he called his mother. I lived by this when Ankhetep was born, healthy and strong. And for the years after it, I told myself Kiya would be my Great Royal Wife; she deserved so for giving me, my Heir. But something held me back."

Aneksi closed her eyes at the Pharaoh's words. It brought back memories that she did not often ponder over but had lasting effects on her future. Three years after her mother's death, the news of Ankhetep's birth was announced and celebrated throughout the lands. Aneksi remembered her father anxiously had expected for a coronation, frustrated that Aneksi was too young for a chance at the throne, being twelve years old. But his fears never solidified as Kiya was never crowned Queen.

The Pharaoh sighed. "Despite having what my father wanted for me -what every Pharaoh needed- I was hopeless." He then moved his right arm and placed a hand on Aneksi's abdomen. Aneksi felt her heart skip a beat and she stopped to look up at him, seeing his eyes were bright and that he was smiling. "I may continue to cherish Ankhetep, but the only mother I want him to see is in you." Aneksi smiled a little and leaned over to kiss the Pharaoh.

"He seems to already have high hopes for me," Aneksi said. The Pharaoh chuckled.

"Yes, I did hear about you two running into each other." The Pharaoh turned to his side to face Aneksi. She allowed him to run his fingers through her short hair, as she no longer felt ashamed of its length. "You are beautiful, Neferkempi."

Aneksi blushed and hid her face to his chest. It was slightly sticky from the heat, but it had the faint smell of the oils she had rubbed into his sensitive skin before going to bed. The Pharaoh smiled and tightened his hold on her.

"Why does me saying those words make you so shy?" he asked.

Aneksi closed her eyes and breathed a sigh of contentment. "Because it only means so much to me when you say it."

PART XVI.

Aneksi blinked her eyes open at the sound of a child's laughter. She pushed herself up on her elbow, seeing through the curtain to the private garden, the shadow of a man holding a child over his head in mock flight.

With a smile, Aneksi dropped back onto the bed and watched the two with sleepy eyes. Aneksi would normally find such a scene disheartening, but she placed a hand over her stomach and knew it would not be long for her, either.

Although it was more than a week since marrying the Pharaoh, their wedding did not mark the first time they had spent a night together. A month prior to the wedding -and two months into their back and forth letters and secret meet-ups at the Tri-God Temple- the Pharaoh had come to her telling her of a trip he would have to make to the Lower lands. It would take weeks for him to return if the conditions were right. Aneksi did not know his name, who his family was, or if he truly loved her, but that night she was too deeply moved by his abrupt departure that she asked neither of those things.

Only her father knew; she did not want to tell the Pharaoh so soon, just in case the signs were too early.

Aneksi's eyelids slowly shut, but before she could touch sleep again, someone thundered into the chamber. Aneksi's eyes shot open and she saw Ankhetep trying to climb onto the bed while looking over his shoulder at the approaching Pharaoh from the garden.

"Oh!"

Ankhetep's eyes widened at the sight of Aneksi. He clamped a hand over his mouth and looked over his shoulder again.

"Are you hiding from your father?" she whispered. He nodded.

"Yes! I must look for somewhere he will not expect to find me. Will you help me?"

Aneksi smiled and nodded, lifting the bedsheets to invite him in.

"Hide under here, he won't think to find you with me."

Just as the Pharaoh drew the curtain to enter, Ankhetep

slipped under the linen covers.

"Ah, you're awake," the Pharaoh said walking across the painted tiles to the bed. Aneksi sat upright to accept his kiss to her forehead. "Good morning, Neferkempi." She smiled.

"Yes, how could I sleep when you and your son have so much fun without me?" Aneksi said.

"So, you have seen him? I closed my eyes for mere moments and he disappeared." Aneksi feigned a loud yawn to cover up Ankhetep's giggle.

"Forgive me, I didn't see where he went. Perhaps he ran off somewhere in expectation that you would follow after."

"Mmm, yes, you may be right." The Pharaoh kicked off his sandals and got onto the bed, edging closer to her. "He wouldn't mind waiting a little, would he?"

Aneksi stiffened as he neared, feeling Ankhetep press closer to her body to ensure the Pharaoh did not touch him.

"You know what," Aneksi quickly said, laying a hand over the Pharaoh's lips, "I do not feel like myself right now. Another time?"

"Is it because-" the Pharaoh began, before grabbing the bed sheets and throwing it away. Aneksi let out a surprised squeak and Ankhetep buried his face in her waist. "-A certain someone is with us?"

Aneksi covered her face in shame at being caught so easily and the Pharaoh threw his head back and laughed. Ankhetep turned to show his face but still held onto Aneksi.

"How did you know I was here, Father?"

The Pharaoh smiled. "Didn't I teach you about taking notice of smaller details?" Ankhetep's brow crease deepened. "Neferkempi had her arm around something by her waist," the Pharaoh explained. "It was clear she was protecting something."

Aneksi lowered her hand from her face and received a quick, teasing kiss to the cheek from the Pharaoh for doing so.

"Oh." Ankhetep turned his head to look at Aneksi and then back. "Father, how do I address her?" The Pharaoh patted his knee and the boy let go of Aneksi to sit on his father's lap.

"You call your half-sisters' mothers Lady, followed by their name. But I want you to call Neferkempi 'Your Highness.'" The boy nodded solemnly. Aneksi held her breath at the Pharaoh's request. If she was not merely a consort like the other wives, that would only mean- "She will be, after all, my Great Royal Wife."

Ankhetep cocked his head to a side. "Mother said that

was her title."

The Pharaoh flicked Ankhetep's forehead. The boy frowned and placed both his hands on the afflicted area, pouting.

"How many times must I tell you my orders are above all else?" the Pharaoh said. "Who am I?"

"You are the Pharaoh, united leader of the Upper and Lower lands, the descendant of the gods, and my father."

"Exactly so, Ankhetep. Is there anyone whose words are more truthful and respected than my own?"

"No, Father."

"And have I told you to call you mother 'Your Highness'?"

"No, Father."

"That's right. Now go back to your mother and have your servants ready you for breakfast."

Ankhetep nodded again and hopped off the Pharaoh's knee to slide down the inclined bed. Both Aneksi and the Pharaoh jumped at the sight of him hitting against the footboard, but before either could do or say anything, Ankhetep ran out of the chamber, exiting through the private garden.

Aneksi made a move to do the same when the Pharaoh

caught her by the waist.

"And where do you think you are off to?" he whispered into her neck. Aneksi closed her eyes briefly.

"Truly, I do not feel like myself," she said, gently moving the Pharaoh's arm from her hips. Aneksi stood up and began rinsing her face with the cold water in the basin by the bed. After sitting upright, something in her lower abdomen had begun to twist and turn.

The Pharaoh moved back, frowning. "Is it your stomach? It pains you again."

Aneksi glanced over at the Pharaoh, wondering if she should laugh at his assumption or be grateful he made it. During their courting months, the Pharaoh was all too aware of when Aneksi's body was causing her to bleed, as the pain often made her too weak to get out of bed. But more evidently, she was forbidden from entering the Temple grounds when she was menstruating.

"Yes," she answered in a low voice. Aneksi heard the Pharaoh sigh as he stood up. He scratched his neck, looking away.

"I'll make sure the physicians have the medicine you need for it."

She smiled. "No need, I would like to visit Meryt about it

123

before breakfast," Aneksi said.

The Pharaoh nodded. "Of course. I'll see you at the dining hall."

Ekmati had his arms folded across his chest, frowning deeply. Meryt glanced at him and then back to Aneksi's confused face.

"Is there something wrong?" Aneksi asked, her voice wavering just the slightest. She was gripping the edge of the bed; grateful no one was at this end of the medicinal chamber.

"Not exactly," Meryt started.

"Am I not healthy enough to carry?"

"No, you are," Meryt answered, "very healthy."

"Then what is it? Why do you act as if this news is something to be concerned about?"

Meryt's voice lowered considerably as she spoke. "Grandfather told me Lady Kiya also came by this morning for the same reason you are here."

Aneksi shook her head, blinking furiously.

"I don't understand, there is no way the Pharaoh and she-"

"No, no, of course not," Meryt said quickly. "She was

several months pregnant already. She had it hidden from many of our servants, otherwise, we would have been the first to know. The only reason she came here this morning was to request for the results of our trial medicine."

Aneksi furrowed her brows. "Results for what? What are you experimenting?"

Ekmati took a step forward to answer.

"We have been working with the High Priest of Hathor, Amenhath, and are in the midst of creating a tonic that will guarantee the birth of a son."

PART XVII.

With breakfast beginning, Aneksi did her best not to stare hate in Kiya's way. She did not want her child to learn hatred so early in its life, regardless if the hate was just. Ekmati had told her they had turned down Kiya because the tests had proven harmful, causing premature and stillborn births, as well as painful infections to the women they had tested on.

"Neferkempi, eat," was the Pharaoh's only words to her. Aneksi pursed her lips, lifting a slice of bread imbedded with nuts and drizzled with honey.

Not only was she upset she did not know when to tell the Pharaoh she was with child, but also because whenever she was able to tell him, it would be loomed over by the news of Kiya's own pregnancy. Kiya had stolen Aneksi's most precious moment from her and she could not forgive her for that.

After the meal, the Pharaoh left on his own to meet with his viziers regarding Palace renovations. Aneksi was on her way to her consort chamber when Rai stopped her.

"My Lady, I was just told your presence was requested by Lady Ahset and Lady Akhara." Aneksi stared at Rai, speechless. Why would the two stoic consorts of the Pharaoh wish to see her? What could they possibly want from her?

"Did they specify when I should present myself?" Aneksi finally asked.

"The servant only said immediately."

Aneksi's shoulders sagged just a bit before she nodded and allowed Ri to lead her to their chambers. She should not jump to any negative conclusions so fast. Perhaps the two wanted to make amends for something or simply wished to invite her over for a cup of beer and talk. But the closer Aneksi was to their chamber, the more she fretted and thought it was a mistake to visit them.

Upon entering the chamber, Aneksi felt a chill sweep through her. The chamber itself was an unusual beautiful: it was full of gold-threaded rugs, silk curtains, hanging cowrie shell pendants, beds shrouded in canopy nets, and had large depictions of Horus along the walls. The chamber was twice as large as its normal size; Aneksi could only assume it was because the two half-sisters agreed to join their chambers to create this.

Ahset and Akhara were lying casually on their elbows atop the two black sofas on either wall of the chamber. Servants fanned them with large peacock feathers. It was difficult for Aneksi to distinguish who was who, for the two consort-sisters dressed and had their servants paint their faces the same, but Aneksi's only reference was that Ahset was older and had more creases along her forehead and mouth that the makeup could not hide.

Overall, their appearance reminded Aneksi of beached crocodiles nested with plovers on their heads along the Nile, waiting for their prey to come near. Aneksi straightened and took a seat by the door.

"Now that the Pharaoh has married each daughter from the house of the gods," Ahset began, sitting upright. She waved away her servant before continuing; "He must, by law, name the Great Royal Wife by the next new moon festival."

Aneksi furrowed her brows, but kept silent, unsure of what to reply with.

127

"You see, Neferkempi-" Aneksi wrinkled her nose at Akhara's use of her nickname. "-The Pharaoh spends a night with each of his consorts once he meets with his viziers about the coronation. We want you to decline this offer."

"What?" Aneksi felt her blood begin to boil at her words. "Each of us has a duty to our lineage. Do not expect me to be so compliant."

"One might assume a link between your arrival at this Palace and the Heir Prince's illness," Akhara said, running a hand through her dark hair.

Aneksi felt her heart lurch to her throat. Was she being threatened?

"By Ma'at, the truth of the matter is that our crop fields are failing," Ahset interrupted, narrowing her eyes at Akhara. Aneksi turned to look at her. "One of us," she continued, indicating herself and her half-sister, "must become Great Royal Wife. Because when the Pharaoh sends his viziers to collect the biennial taxes from our people, they will starve. Only Akhara and I know what we must do to bring aid to our villages."

"Why me?" Aneksi said.

Ahset leaned back into the sofa, resting an arm on its headrest.

"We do not expect any of the other consorts to have a chance at the throne as you do."

After a stretch of silence, Aneksi glanced from one consort to the other. It was a noble cause; Aneksi knew her father oversaw many fields along the northern tip of the Nile where they received most of their income. If any were to fail, it would hinder their offerings to the Palace. But could she give up her right as Great Royal Wife for them?

"Relax and drink with us," Ahset finally said with a smile. "Let us discuss this further without worries."

Aneksi looked away, feeling her spine crawl with unease. One of their servants walked forward to fan her and another two servants carried a tray of silver, beer-filled goblets. Looking at it, Aneksi absently laid a hand over her abdomen.

"Forgive me, but I should be on my way," she said, rising from her seat to take a step toward the door. "I will consider your offer and think of the families who serve you."

"We don't expect anything less," Akhara said, taking a cup from one of the trays and gulping down its contents. She set the cup down and motioned for Aneksi to go. "Go on now."

Aneksi turned around and stepped out of the chamber as fast as she could. Rai looked up at her when she exited. She turned to face him.

"If they ever request my audience again, don't notify of it to me," Aneksi said in a low voice. He nodded.

With a sigh, Aneksi made her way to the medicinal chambers to see Lithra. She had brought her good council before and Aneksi desperately needed it now.

"You've always been considerate of others' needs," Lithra said after hearing Aneksi's ordeal. "I find this a decision you know the answer to."

"But my father will be furious with me."

"This is not about your father, Ani. And weren't you ready to elope with another man when he wanted you married to the Pharaoh?" Aneksi stared down at her hands. "Ani are you telling me you *want* to be Great Royal Wife?" Lithra asked, awe in her voice.

"Is it so wrong of me to?" Aneksi shot back. Seeing Lithra raise her eyebrows, she added, "I do feel that the Pharaoh regards me differently than the rest of the-"

Aneksi was cut off by a slap to the face.

Rai jumped, startled by the sudden movement, and grabbed Aneksi's hand to pull her away from Lithra. Aneksi stumbled back into Rai's chest, holding her cheek.

"Lithra...?"

Lithra's face was red and the hand she used to hit Aneksi with was shaking. Tears were forming in her eyes.

"I thought you were selfless and caring, Ani."

"At your word I will have her hand cut off for her actions," Rai said, letting go of Aneksi's hand to unsheathe the dagger at his hip.

Lithra inhaled sharply and gazed at Aneksi with large, blue eyes. But Aneksi no longer recognized them. She turned away, facing her back to the two.

The words slipped out: "Do it."

Aneksi rushed out of the hall, but not before she heard Lithra scream.

PART XVIII.

"Aneksi, you did what?"

Meryt's dark brown eyes were wide with alarm. Aneksi covered her face with her hands, bending over. She had sought Meryt after leaving the medicinal hall, not to be told she was in the right for what she had done, but to confess a crime she had committed against her friend.

"By Ma'at, I don't know what came over me," Aneksi mumbled, grateful that Meryt had told Thut to leave when she arrived. "I was just so frustrated by her attitude towards

131

me this whole time. And then she went ahead and raised her hand to me? I couldn't understand."

"The gods help you," Meryt said in sympathy, laying a hand on Aneksi's shoulder. "Do you intend to keep her as your servant?"

"No, she will not keep me as her friend," Aneksi whispered. "I don't think she will ever serve me as she once did."

Meryt shook her head in disbelief.

"I would say your friendship was lost the moment she thought to strike you or even found the audacity to think she was above you. Such a slave, or anyone for that matter, is dangerous to keep at your side. Some good has come of this."

Aneksi shut her eyes, feeling her chest ache. Her relationship with Lithra had unraveled so quickly after coming to the Palace. Their love and trust for one another was now nothing but a vague memory to her.

Perhaps that was why she felt no remorse in ordering for Lithra's hand to be cut off.

"Don't stress yourself so much, Aneksi, you have a child to think of," Meryt finally said. Aneksi remained silent. Meryt sighed. "Alright, let's talk of something else." Meryt paused a moment and then suddenly sat upright. "Would you rather have me speak about Lady Kiya?"

Aneksi looked up. "What news of her do you have?"

Meryt adjusted the beads in her hair, weaving one strand of her hair into a temporary braid. "Grandfather believes she is nearing the last months before labor."

"So soon?" Aneksi asked, raising her eyebrows. "Did you not say before she visited you only once? She doesn't look like a woman who is halfway through a pregnancy." Meryt shook her head.

"She receives her medical care from the Temple of Isis; typically, those who fear complications visit us. And to be truthful, I could only imagine that Isis has blessed Lady Kiya for this. We knew nothing of Prince Ankhetep's pregnancy until her labor began, so I assume it was only desperation on her part that gave away this one." Meryt paused, watching Aneksi, before laying a hand on her shoulder and standing up. "I know I don't quite understand how you could feel in such a situation, but always have hope. Now come, we should ready for our midday meal."

Instead of retreating to her consort chamber that night -as expected of a menstruating consort of the Pharaoh- Aneksi decided she would tell the truth to him. There was no point

133

in waiting, and she also did not want the Pharaoh to be misled about her condition.

Tonight was especially cold, and several candles hung above the bed and along the walls in addition to the normal two by the chamber door. The servants had also brought in several more layers of bedsheets to stave away the cooler breezes from the garden.

"Aneksi?" She looked over at the doorway to see the Pharaoh closing the door behind him. "You know you are not to be with me during this time," he said, not meeting her gaze.

"Yes, I do know." Aneksi gripped her hands, seeing the Pharaoh remained where he stood.

His downcast face was illuminated by the candles on either side of the door, flickering light from the gold piercings on his ear across the chamber.

"But Meryt confirmed my pains are not due to...that."

The Pharaoh took a step forward, his eyebrows furrowed in worry. His right arm was lifted half-way, a frozen, unfinished act.

"Is there something wrong then? Dear gods don't tell me you are not incapable of bearing children." Aneksi exhaled lightly, looking briefly down at her stomach below the several layers draped over her.

"No, it's quite the opposite. I am with child."

The Pharaoh blinked and then he smiled.

"I can't believe it!"

Aneksi felt her face flush as he walked towards her, his smile growing into a mischievous grin. He pulled back the covers, settling down between Aneksi's legs to place an ear to her lower abdomen. Aneksi inhaled sharply and looked away, drawing in her legs and shifting them farther apart to allow him more room. She felt her nightgown slip above her knees and tilted her head to watch the Pharaoh from the corner of her eyes.

"How long have you known this?" the Pharaoh asked in a low voice, running a hand over her exposed left leg. Aneksi closed her eyes, exhaling slowly.

"Only a few days."

The Pharaoh looked up at Aneksi.

"Ankhetep would love a little brother," he whispered. Aneksi pressed her shut eyes tighter.

"I don't want the day to come when you have to choose between my son or Lady Kiya's son to take after you."

Aneksi felt the Pharaoh turn his head and sigh loudly, his breath fanning where the nightgown had accumulated by her inner thigh.

"My First Wife is pregnant again," he confessed, lament clear in his voice. Aneksi's eyes shot open and her body tensed. When did he find out?

The Pharaoh kept his gaze on Aneksi's thigh.

"I learned she was four months due the morning I came back from the Lower Lands," the Pharaoh said, answering Aneksi's unspoken question. "I ordered that she tell no one for the sake of you not finding out." He moved his thumb across Aneksi's leg. He stopped when he reached her knee and his eyes became stern. "That night and every night for some weeks, I had asked the gods to take the child away from her. But the gods came for Ankhetep."

Aneksi laid a hand on the Pharaoh's shaven head, her voice low.

"I don't believe the gods would spite you in this way. After all, Ankhetep fell ill much later."

The Pharaoh shook his head. "It aches my heart still. It was wrong of me to pray for the death of an innocent child, as a man and as a father. I know that now." Aneksi felt a hot tear soak into the light fabric of her nightgown.

"Look at me." Aneksi forced the Pharaoh's head to her direction, seeing the tears in his eyes and streaking down his face. Aneksi gently wiped them away with her fingers, giving him a small smile. "You are not to blame for Prince Ankhetep's illness."

"How can you be assured of that?"

"Because the gods blessed Ankhetep with a quick recovery and gave you this." Aneksi lowered her hand from his face to place it over her stomach. "How can either be a punishment?"

"Neferkempi," the Pharaoh said sitting up.

He firmly placed his hands on either side of Aneksi's hips and leaned forward to kiss her gently. He then drew away to hoist her onto his lap. Aneksi's legs curled around the Pharaoh's waist as he shrugged off his robe.

"Neferkempi, be my Great Royal Wife," the Pharaoh whispered, looking up at Aneksi with pleading eyes. "I was advised that I perform the ritual cycle before I named you, but this," he said, pressing Aneksi's lower abdomen to his, "is decision enough that you have always been the right one."

Aneksi bent her head to close the distance between their lips, feeling the Pharaoh's hands travel ever-so-slowly up along her thighs. She did not think twice about Ahset and Akhara's request to know her answer.

PART XIX.

"You're not wearing your father's charm."

Ekmati frowned deeply at Aneksi's bowed head.

Aneksi had woken up with a fever and the Pharaoh had her taken immediately to the High Priest. When Ekmati saw the golden pendant in her hands -not around her neck- he pulled her aside into a separate chamber. Ekmati had told her there that her father had explicitly mentioned to him of the nightmare spell being cast upon her from her kidnapper, thus his inquiry of it.

"It slipped off," she whispered, her face heating up at what she was implying to the High Priest of Sekhmet. But the elder only wrinkled his nose at her response.

"You've allowed yourself to be endangered by this spell from being heedless of your actions. This fever could very well have hurt your unborn child; how severely, I cannot say for certain. I advise that you test yourself again to make sure you are still carrying the child."

Aneksi lifted her head briefly to nod, swallowing hard. She did not know much about sorcery, only that it was volatile, and her father did not allow her to read his scrolls about it.

"Should I let my father know?"

"For now, no. Unless you require something stronger for protection, come back to me and I will send for Kairunamete to make any adjustments." Aneksi hesitated, before speaking up again.

"Shouldn't the Pharaoh be made aware of what is happening to me?"

Ekmati folded his arms over his chest, leaning back against his heels.

"No."

"But-"

"No." Ekamti's voice was sharp. "I will tell him your fever was a symptom of the child's growth. Now come this way."

Ekmati walked over to retrieve a clay vase and handed it to Aneksi before exiting the room to bring back a cloth sack. In it was a handful of soil with barley and wheat seeds. Aneksi would have to urinate into the vase, which would later be poured onto the soil. If either of the two seeds grew, it would mean she was still pregnant. Her last test had caused the barley seeds to sprout, which, Ekmati assured meant she would have a baby boy. If the same could occur this time, it would mean the gods had truly given her a son.

Aneksi did was needed of her and was told to return in the next few weeks. She was bathed, dressed, and then sent for breakfast. Among those to dine with them were the Pharaoh's viziers.

Aneksi immediately knew why.

The wives were instructed to stand side-by-side, facing the Pharaoh where he sat. Their children were standing to the Pharaoh's right and the viziers to his left. Ankhetep was present with his older sisters this time. He waved to Aneksi but received a glare from his mother, forcing him to lower his hand. The servants lined the walls on either sides and scribes had their desks brought in. All hushed when the Pharaoh raised a hand to speak.

"I, son of Amanrakh and grandson of Tyamun, and with the favor of the gods, name the daughter of Lord-Priest Kairunamete of the Tri-God Temple to be my Great Royal Wife."

One of the viziers spoke. "Please step forward."

Aneksi felt the stares of every man, woman, and child her way. The coldest of them all belonged to Ahset and Akhara. But she ignored them, walking over to the Pharaoh with her head held high.

They thought she would be compliant because she had done nothing to their daughters' maltreatment of Thut and Freyi. But Aneksi knew now that once she was Queen, she could bring change to the Palace atmosphere. Her children would not have to grow up under such harsh conditions nor would the children already in the Palace have to suffer through them.

The Royal Scribe offered Aneksi and the Pharaoh a quill to sign their names at the bottom of the scroll to document the crowning. Aneksi nodded, taking the reed pen and leaned down, signing her name. The Pharaoh placed his left arm around her as he stood beside her, taking the quill from her to sign below her name.

Once done, breakfast resumed. An extra table had been brought in to accommodate the viziers while Aneksi took her seat by the Pharaoh at their table.

The children stepped down to sit across their mothers as ordained, but Ankhetep gazed up at the Pharaoh and his Great Royal Wife with large, brown eyes.

"May I dine with you, Father, and Your Highness?"

They were speaking through the Master of Servants' procedural speech.

Aneksi glanced at the Pharaoh, who had also turned to look at her for an answer. She smiled and leaned over to pat Ankhetep's shaven head. She knew Kiya would be more than livid if he dined with them the same time she had been denied the title of Great Royal Wife.

"You should eat with your mother," Aneksi said, taking her hand back. Ankhetep frowned but nodded.

"What do you say now, Ankhetep?" the Pharaoh asked, an eyebrow raised. Ankhetep squared his shoulders.

"Your decision is a command I will adhere to, Your Highness."

"Good, you may go now."

Aneksi watched Ankhetep jump down the steps and take his seat. She did not look Kiya's way.

"He doesn't need to be so formal," Aneksi said, turning to address the Pharaoh. "I prefer him not to be."

"That may be so, but he still has yet to know you. Until then, I would like for him to show you the highest respect." Aneksi nodded and they began their meal.

When the servants carried the trays to them, she smiled, seeing that the selection of food being offered to her was greater than usual. Aneksi was no longer eating for herself, but for the future of the Pharaoh's child within her.

"I was planning a proper arrangement for you and Ankhetep to be acquainted with one another," the Pharaoh said, washing his hands in the silver bowl offered to him. "Perhaps this afternoon?"

Aneksi nodded. "I look forward to it."

"As I do," the Pharaoh said with a smile.

They were to meet in the portico of the Royal chambers.

The portico was an enormous, high ceilinged chamber that branched out to the Pharaoh's other places of rest, including the private chamber, a solar chamber, a musician's and dance chamber, a royal lavatory, as well as small corridors that lead to storage chambers filled with boxed goods and food. The columns were built of wood and plaster, painted over in gold and white. The chamber consisted of expensive cushions, wood carved chairs, and ornate-legged tables that held statues and oil lamps. Thick drapery hung along the walls and windows, and there was a side stairwell that led to a small balcony.

Aneksi was seated upon one of the cushions, wringing her hands in anticipation. Ankhetep had shown a positive interest in her thus far, but Aneksi still worried if it would be enough for what was needed of her.

The Pharaoh had left earlier to escort Kiya to the Temple of Isis where she would remain for the birth of her second child. Until Kiya's return, Aneksi was given the task to watch over Ankhetep. Ankhetep's aunt, Epehshert, one of the

Pharaoh's half-sisters, also Ankhetep's wet nurse, would aid her.

"Here we are."

Aneksi looked over by the doorway to see Epehshert walk in with Ankhetep at her side. The boy was holding her hand, but upon seeing Aneksi, let go and raced over. His aunt followed after.

"Your Highness!" he exclaimed. Aneksi smiled at his enthusiasm. "Father told me you would accompany me until my mother returns. Do you know where and why she is going? Or when she will return?"

Aneksi motioned for him to sit at her side. He complied.

"Your mother needs to be with Isis right now," Aneksi began.

"Why? Can she not reach Isis at the Temple here?"

"Yes, she can, but your mother must be guarded properly-"

"Why? Is there a threat she faces here?"

Epehshert shook her head. "Ankhetep. Let Her Highness speak."

Aneksi smiled shyly at her sister-in-law in thanks. But she admired Ankhetep's curiosity and demand. If he could express them properly, she was sure he would grow up to be a good Pharaoh.

"You are going to have a baby brother or sister, Ankhetep, so your mother will be staying at the Temple of Isis to be protected from evil spirits. Your grandfather will make sure of that."

Ankhetep jumped off the cushion to walk about, a hand on his chin. Aneksi smiled at the sight. She knew he had learned it from the Pharaoh.

"What are you thinking about so deeply, Ankhetep?" she asked.

He turned to face Aneksi.

"Mother did not consult me on this matter," he said, concerned. "She did not ask for my thoughts if I wanted another sibling."

"Ankhetep, some things only the gods have control over," Aneksi said with a small laugh. "This is one of them."

"Oh."

At his crestfallen look, Aneksi smiled and said, "So tell me, would you prefer a brother or sister?"

"A brother," he answered immediately. Aneksi's smile faltered. The Pharaoh did indeed know his son.

"But why a brother?"

"My older sisters do not speak with me and they look at

me with cold expressions. Also, they do not play with me." he frowned. "I do not want another sister."

Aneksi thought a moment, placing her hands in her lap.

"Had you the chance to play and speak with her whenever you wished, would you want a sister?"

"Yes," Ankhetep said with a nod. Aneksi smiled.

"Alright. Now then, what shall we play?"

The Pharaoh returned to the Palace a few hours past sundown. Aneksi and the other consorts had their evening meal already, leaving the Pharaoh to dine on his own. He entered the private chamber where Aneksi was already sleeping under the covers.

The Pharaoh smiled and settled himself beside her. He ran his hand through her short hair over and over until he himself grew weary of his thoughts.

The search for Aneksi's kidnapper only led to seven dead bodies of a young girl, a male toddler, an older woman, and the four guards who had taken her there. It left the Pharaoh and his court officials with even less a trail to find the culprit. He feared that he would have to drop the search entirely.

But for now, nothing else seemed amiss and the Pharaoh hoped to keep it that way.

PART XX.

Nearly two months had passed since the Pharaoh had named Aneksi Great Royal Wife. The public ceremony would be held sometime in the following two weeks to have it coincide with a new moon and the biennial tax collection. Priests from the Lower Lands were also invited and their coming would mark the coronation.

"Your dress will need some alterations," Meryt said, waving to one of the servants, "to accommodate the child's growth."

Aneksi turned to a side, looking at herself in the mirror another servant held up for her. She was wearing a light cotton robe, with a string loosely tied below her breast, before it split away to expose her lower body. Below the open robe she wore a short underskirt. Above all this, she wore a gold and turquoise collar that spread over her breast and along her shoulders. With her hair growing back at a considerable rate, Aneksi's now shoulder-length black locks were intricately weaved into her headdresses.

It was the casual morning attire of a queen.

The necklace Kairunamęte gave her to ward off her dreams had been adjusted to a bracelet, to accommodate any activities or jewelry preference.

147

Aneksi placed a hand over her stomach, feeling the very noticeable bump. The test she had taken in caution had come back positive, with the sprouting of the barley seeds, affirming the prediction of a son once more. Ekmati had also told her she would be able to hear the child's heartbeat now.

"But I thought I would only need clothing adjustments when I near halfway," Aneksi said, raising her arms to allow a servant to measure her waist with knotted rope above and below her stomach. "By the time the ceremony is conducted, I will only near my fourth month."

Meryt smiled a little.

"That's true, but I am inclining to believe something may be different with your pregnancy."

Aneksi's eyes widened. "What do you mean?"

"Nothing worrisome, I assure you." Seeing Aneksi's still concerned face, Meryt shook her head to explain. "My father has been collecting data from our Temple and the Temple of Hathor from the mothers who visit for blessings. My grandfather and I have been working to match these notes and label similarities on the child's outcome with the mother's pregnancy process. I cannot be for certain, but I do feel you fall into one of the categories."

Aneksi dropped her arms and turned about to have the

servant measure the whole of her thighs.

"What category do I fall under?"

Before Meryt could answer, the Pharaoh walked into the chamber. The servants immediately stepped away from Aneksi and she walked towards the Pharaoh to accept his good morning kiss.

"You seem much better than most mornings," he said, smiling down at her. Aneksi felt her cheeks flush as she smiled back up at him.

"I do feel it, too."

"You're beautiful," he whispered.

"I'm barely dressed," Aneksi corrected, but she dropped her gaze, abashed.

The Pharaoh placed his hand over Aneksi's stomach.

"All the more beautiful, then."

Neither had acknowledged Meryt, who sat silently in the chamber. But upon seeing her, the Pharaoh withdrew his arm and cleared his throat.

"It's time for breakfast, Neferkempi, so please ready yourself."

Aneksi pouted and tugged on the Pharaoh's robe.

"Perhaps we can dine by ourselves in the portico," she suggested. "I don't feel like eating in public."

The Pharaoh's face broke into a grin.

"Of course."

After breakfast had been served privately, Aneksi stretched herself along one of the sofas, draping her legs across the Pharaoh's lap. The curtains were drawn and tied, letting the breezes cool the warm air in the chamber.

The Pharaoh had his eyes closed and head bent back, leaning against the wall.

"A priest from the Temple of Isis arrived last night," he said. Aneksi turned, looking at him. She had not heard of anything of the sort from any of the servants or from Rai.

"What news did he bring?"

The Pharaoh turned to meet her gaze.

"I have another prince."

Aneksi felt her heart skip a beat. She looked away, staring at the open window from across the chamber. A bird flew past. She could not be certain, but it looked to be a crow.

"What have they named him?" she asked out of courtesy, her voice now in a whisper.

"Isiskah did not reveal the name in his letter. I was told I would learn of it when the baby is brought here later today."

Aneksi nodded and kept quiet. She was unsure if her displeasure came from the fact that if she ever had a son, his chances to be Pharaoh were slim, or if the news itself was upsetting to hear. Or if it was because her head had suddenly seized with pain.

Rai took a step forward and announced that Ankhetep and his wet nurse Epehshert had arrived. The Pharaoh glanced at Aneksi. She closed her eyes briefly but nodded. As Rai went to allow the two in, Aneksi slowly raised herself to an upright position.

The Pharaoh stood up to kiss her forehead and patted Ankhetep's head on his way out of the portico.

"How do you fare, Your Highness?" Ankhetep asked, standing tall before her. He had a carved slingshot in his hand. Aneksi smiled.

For the months Kiya was not here, Aneksi watched Ankhetep play. Sometimes she joined him when she did not feel too fatigued. Other times Epehshert had servant boys play with him. Though Ankhetep was governed by formalities and rules of court, he was still nothing more than a child.

"By the gods, I'm doing well." Ankhetep nodded solemnly. "Say, Ankhetep, would you like to hear a secret?" At this, the boy's expression dissolved into a grin.

"Yes!"

Aneksi gently placed both her hands upon his head and

turned to have his ear brush against the bulge in her stomach.

For a moment Ankhetep furrowed his eyebrows, unable to 'hear' the secret Aneksi spoke of. But then he heard the small thumps echoing within Aneksi and his eyes widened, and he gripped her wrists.

Ankhetep looked up at Aneksi and whispered, "Has your heart moved, Your Highness?"

Aneksi let out a laugh, and Epehshert hid her giggles behind a hand. Rai grinned.

"No, Ankhetep, my heart is still here." Aneksi leaned over, motioning for him to lay an ear to her chest.

Upon hearing her heartbeat, Ankhetep frowned.

"How do you have two hearts?" he asked, sitting down on the tiled floor. The slingshot was now resting beside him.

"One is mine, yes," Aneksi said, "but the other is not."

"Whose is it, then?"

"It belongs to a brother or sister of yours." Ankhetep tilted his head, his eyes narrowed in thought.

"I'm to have *another* brother or sister?" he asked.

"Yes. However, this sibling of yours shares only half of your blood."

Ankhetep placed a finger to his chin. "Am I still allowed to play with this brother or sister?"

"I should hope so," Aneksi said with a smile. "Your mother may not be fond of the idea."

Ankhetep picked up his slingshot.

"Father says I am the Crown Prince. If I am to be the next King, I will not always take orders from my mother. Shall we play now, Your Highness?"

Aneksi smiled and stood up to walk after Ankhetep, who had run out of the portico already. She faltered in her step, but before she could fall, a concerned Rai caught her. Aneksi shook her head, blinking furiously to sharpen her vision.

"I'm fine. A small headache; it's nothing too troubling." Rai let her go and watched her take Epehshert's hand to steady herself.

When Kiya arrived that afternoon, she did so with a procession of priests from the Lower Lands behind her. The Pharaoh stood at the front of the Palace with his guards in position, eager to see his second son.

Kiya looked no different than she had when she left, but one could almost say she looked more beautiful than before.

She wore a brilliant white robe, its edges sewn in with fine golden thread, and wearing the white-feathered and blue turquoise headdress representing her father's Temple.

153

Stitched into the center of her garment was also a lotus flower.

Kiya stepped down with the help of the guards and turned back to take her son from her servant who was still within the six-man palanquin. She dipped low before the Pharaoh. Once at her full height, she offered him the baby to hold. The Pharaoh smiled and took the child, his eyes flittering across the small bundle's features.

"His name?" the Pharaoh whispered, not looking up.

"Ka-Rae. The soul of Ra."

The Pharaoh nodded, glancing up at the sunny sky, before turning around and entering the Palace. Kiya followed after.

Inside was a prepared feast for the mother and prince. All consorts were present, as were their children. The Lower Lands priests were also included in the celebration.

Upon seeing his mother, Ankhetep raced over from Aneksi's side to greet her. However, the moment he did, Kiya clenched her hand around his wrist and did not let him go. Though Kiya was beautiful and had just brought the Palace a prince, with Aneksi as the Great Royal Wife, she commanded the attention of almost every eye still.

The Pharaoh held the baby boy in his arms, admiring

him, for most of the feast. He even let Aneksi hold Ka-Rae, much to Kiya's displeasure. Many of the servants buzzed with curiosity at the new prince, stealing glances his way. Ankhetep frowned during the duration of the feast, unable to leave his mother's side, nor was he able to look at the awaited brother of his.

Excitement over the new prince continued into the night. The Pharaoh retreated to his private chamber with Aneksi and the child. Ka-Rae was a quiet babe, and he simply stared up as the two coddled him. Ka-Rae had a hazelnut complexion, a mix of his mother and father's tones, and his large, dark eyes were surely from his mother. But beyond that, Aneksi saw no resemblance in the boy -and hoped she would never- to Kiya.

"Will he take residence at the Nursery?" Aneksi asked, absently adjusting the child's clothes.

"Yes, I plan on settling Ka-Rae there tomorrow."

Aneksi looked up at the Pharaoh as he lifted the baby and placed him in the makeshift cradle beside the bed.

"Perhaps I'm overthinking, but I feel Ankhetep won't like the idea."

The Pharaoh looked over his shoulder. "Do you think so?"

"I do," Aneksi agreed. "Having someone to play with is Ankhetep's idea of a brother. To change his sleeping chamber for this brother is something I feel Ankhetep hasn't expected and therefore wouldn't be so agreeable to."

With a sigh, the Pharaoh settled back onto the bed with an arm bent over his head and using the other to bring Aneksi to his side. A servant appeared and rocked the child to sleep, unheeded by the two.

"Ankhetep is a growing boy. He'll agree to reason." Aneksi nodded and closed her eyes. She felt the Pharaoh turn his head and kiss her temple. "How is our son doing?"

Opening her eyes, Aneksi placed a hand over the Pharaoh's bare chest, feeling a slight moment of unease at the Pharaoh's quick assumption of their unborn child.

"He brings me much discomfort during the day," she said, "but I would not want it any other way if it means he'll be healthy." The Pharaoh squeezed her shoulders with his arm in affection.

"If he pains you too much, I will have quite a few things to say to him when he is born."

PART XXI.

Meryt rubbed Aneksi's back with a firm hand as the latter

held onto the rim of the bucket and hurled up the contents of her stomach. A servant nearby patted a cooling cloth on her forehead.

"That's enough, now lift your head," Meryt whispered. "The worst is over."

Aneksi spat the last of the bile into the bucket and moved away from it, allowing for two other servants to wash her up. Meryt stood away and waited for them to finish. After, she gave Aneksi an encouraging smile and took Aneksi's hand to escort her back to her consort chamber. Before Aneksi could lie down to rest, Rai knocked, entering soon after.

"An emergency meeting has been called. Your Highness must be present."

With a sigh, Aneksi stood back up and had her servants dress and ready her for public display.

In the throne room, Aneksi took her seat beside the Pharaoh. She gave him a weak smile and he squeezed her hand. Standing before them was Kiya and her guards. On either side of the two monarchs were the Pharaoh's viziers.

The two women refused to look the other in the eyes as Kiya's kneeling guard spoke.

"We have found the culprit who poisoned the Crown Prince, may he live for an eternity," the guard began. Aneksi's eyes widened and the Pharaoh leaned forward in his seat.

"This is good news. Where is he? Show him to me."

The guard stood up and motioned for one of the servants to open the door. The one who did as requested was one of Ahset and Akhara's servants.

Bound by the feet and hands, a young boy was brought before the Pharaoh. The child was blindfolded and gagged. Aneksi's eyes narrowed, feeling some recognition of the boy. She had seen him before. When? Where?

"The jar he possesses had traces of arsenic within it," the guard continued, once again motioning for a servant to bring in the clay jar. There was a large crack on one of its sides.

Aneksi swallowed hard.

He could not be the boy she had seen during her first morning at their private garden, could he?

"We are unsure of how he was able to enter the private chambers of the Palace," the guard said, "and he has revealed no names to a master. My Lady begs you to publicly execute him." Kiya bowed her head at these last words.

The Pharaoh leaned back, hands gripping the edge of his armrests and his lips pressed in a firm line.

"Untie him. Let him see his King."

The guard did as told and Aneksi felt her heart drop. It

was indeed the young boy she had seen. And seeing his fractured jar from having dropped it that morning validated it all the more.

"Your Highness, save me!" the boy suddenly cried out, staring directly at Aneksi. A collective gasp rang through the chamber and Kiya looked up, eyes wide in shock.

Aneksi felt her blood still as the Pharaoh turned to face her.

"Neferkempi?" his voice was barely above a whisper. "Do you know this boy?"

Aneksi looked from the Pharaoh to the child, and then back. Her heart lurched to her throat at the sight of the Pharaoh's open display of pain as he stared at her.

"I do recognize-"

"By Isis, I knew it was you!" Kiya screamed, taking a step forward. Her eyes were blazing with animosity and her hands were clenched to fists at her side. Aneksi flinched. "The day you entered this Palace, my boy fell ill! Our great Pharaoh trusted his own flesh and blood to you these past months, yet you are the one who put Ankhetep's life in danger to begin with! I will have you executed for harming my son, do you hear me?"

The Pharaoh raised a hand to stop her, but Kiya spoke

on.

"I demand she be put to trial!" she shouted, sweeping her arm across the chamber, seeking approval of those present. "My sons are not safe with her! Your love for her as blinded you so much that she sits beside you despite her unthinkable crimes!"

"No, no," Aneksi fumbled for the right words, her heart racing in her chest, as she turned from the Pharaoh to the room of witnesses. The servant had let go of the boy and was standing by the door, while the boy swayed, staring at the gritty floor. Aneksi felt a coldness creeping into her blood, and her breathing falter. "I had no part, I swear- by Ma'at-"

"That's enough." The Pharaoh's voice was sharp and all hushed as he turned away from Aneksi with a hand over his face. Aneksi's shoulders fell and she stared at the Pharaoh in horror at his next words. "As Pharaoh, I uphold the laws of my fathers and ancestors before me. I cannot let my personal feelings hinder justice."

Kiya lifted her head and placed a hand on her hip at his next words.

"Nef- Lady Aneksi will be put to trial regarding any possible association to the Crown Prince's attempted murder tonight," the Pharaoh continued, "As this is a matter of urgency, nothing that has transpired here shall be uttered or recorded beyond this chamber. All of you be on your way."

Kiya took a step back, but her eyes were momentarily glued to Aneksi's shivering frame before she turned up her nose and strode out of the chamber. One of the viziers inquired about the boy's fate as her guards and servants filed out of the throne room after her.

"This child's judgment will be determined once this preliminary case is settled." The Pharaoh glanced at her before forcing himself to look away. As the suspect of her alleged crime, he would be unable to speak or be in relation with her until her trial was over and a verdict passed unanimously between himself and the viziers. "Please escort Nefer-Lady Aneksi away," he said in a low voice.

Aneksi stiffened as Rai approached her with a solemn face. She turned to look back at the Pharaoh as she was guided down the steps, but his face was turned away, his hand over his eyes. Aneksi felt her chest tighten and dread knot in her stomach at the sight.

She was ordered to remain in her consort chamber without outside contact with anyone else until that night. Rai was allowed to enter, but only if it were an emergency regarding her health. Aneksi spent most of the day curled up on the sofa, her eyes shut, and her arms around her waist. Her headdress and jewelry lay strewn on the floor, having torn them off her body, and her makeup smeared from her tears.

Chills swept through her body at the thought of what she would be facing during the trial. If guilty, she would be executed for being an accomplice to Ankhetep's poisoning.

She and her child.

Aneksi looked down at the charm her father had given her. This was no nightmare. It was truly happening.

PART XXII.

There was a knock.

Aneksi barely opened her eyes from the noise when someone lightly stepped into the chamber, carrying a tray of food in hand.

"Lithra...?"

Her slave placed the tray on the small table and sat down at the base of the sofa. She still had bandages along her arms and legs, but they were no longer blood-stained. Aneksi's gaze traveled to the stump of her left hand. She swallowed hard and looked into Lithra's blue eyes.

"I haven't seen you in so long. How could you have forgiven me?"

162

Lithra closed her eyes briefly.

"The servants spoke of how you were accused of poisoning the Crown Prince. How could I not forgive you in your time of need? I know you're innocent, by Ma'at."

Aneksi's lips trembled and her eyes began to water.

"The gods know I missed you," she choked out, reaching out a hand. Lithra smiled a little and took her hand. "I dared not show my face to you fearing you were still upset. I'm so glad to see you're alright."

"That was in the past, Ani. I hope you to forgive me for my recklessness as well." Aneksi nodded. Lithra's smile grew wider. "Thank you, Ani. Now, when did you last eat?" she asked, turning to the tray of food.

Aneksi hesitated. Lithra glanced at her. She let go of Aneksi's hand.

"Shall I have someone test it?"

"Yes, please." Aneksi nodded. It was not that she did not fully trust Lithra, it was merely a precaution her father had penned to her. She could not eat or drink anything without having physically seen someone test it.

Mutely, Rai brought in a passing servant to test the meal. The youth took small bites of the bread and fruits and sips of the water and honey. After washing his hands and no hindrance of his health, Rai escorted him back out.

Aneksi ate the food quickly after, not realizing how hungry she had been. Lithra sat patiently at her side, pouring her more water or offering an extra spoonful of honey. It did not occur to Aneksi to take note of the collar or wristband Lithra wore, after all, they were quite hard to see below the bandages wrapped along her neck and arms.

When Aneksi was finally called for trial, her heart had begun hammering painfully in her chest for the past several minutes. While her initial trial was tonight, it could be months before a unanimous verdict was reached. This would mean her coronation would be postponed and she would have no way to speak with her father or even Meryt. But worst of all, she would have no contact with the Pharaoh.

Aneksi wrinkled her nose and walked through the hall with a suddenly aching head. Thinking it to be a symptom of her pregnancy, Aneksi placed a hand over her stomach, gritting her teeth. She could not show any weakness when giving her testimony.

On her way, Palace guards followed Aneksi to ensure she did not have any contact with anyone. At one point, Aneksi's vision blurred and she pressed against the side of the wall to steady herself. She closed her eyes and breathed deeply before setting off again, wondering why Rai had not come to aid her this time.

Aneksi found herself escorted back in the throne room. This time, scribes were seated along the walls and one at the foot of the thrones. A curtain had been put up to hide the identities of those who would judge her: The Great Kenbet.

It would include the Pharaoh, as well as his viziers and any other regional Kenbet the Pharaoh wished to have to judge beside him. Many of the candles had been blown out, leaving only the hissing sconce behind the Kenbet alight to throw their shadows across the chamber.

Kiya was standing to her left, staring straight ahead at the anonymous, seated men.

"Your Highness, Great Royal Wife of the Pharaoh, daughter of Lord Priest Kairunamete, Lady Aneksi, and Royal Consort of the Pharaoh, Daughter of High Priest Isiskah, Lady Kiya, place your right hand over your left shoulder," a voice said from behind the curtain. A drop of sweat ran down the side of Aneksi's face as she did so. Kiya followed suit. "Together, repeat these words: I swear upon Ma'at that the words I speak hereon after are only of the Truth."

"I swear-" Aneksi paused a moment to clear her throat before regaining composure to continue after Kiya. "-Upon

Ma'at that the words I speak hereon after are only of the Truth."

"Should anything I say be discovered to be false, I shall willingly accept the punishment of Liars."

Aneksi swallowed as they spoke, forcing down the bile and fear welling up in her throat.

"Should anything I say be discovered to be false, I shall willingly accept the punishment of Liars."

"You may lower your hand." Aneksi exhaled and slowly moved her hand to her side. Kiya glanced Aneksi's way and did the same. "Your Highness, you are accused by the Royal Consort Lady Kiya in aiding the poisoning of Crown Prince Ankhetep..."

The rest of his words muddled together in Aneksi's ears. She shook her head slightly and blinked to clear mind. She felt something inside her move, and with it, came a shot of searing pain.

Aneksi gasped and bent over a bit, clenching her hands.

"...What do you have to say in defense to these allegations?"

Aneksi looked up, breathing hard.

"I have nothing to do with them," she choked out. Aneksi inhaled deeply, seeing from the corner of her eyes Kiya frown, but waited for her to continue. "I saw the boy only once-" a sharp pain ripped through her abdomen and this time, Aneksi could not hide it. She let out a hiss and bent over, wincing with her hand over her stomach.

One of the shadows stood up at the sight but was pulled back to his seat.

"Is Ma'at punishing you for speaking falsehood after your oath?" another voice asked from behind the screen.

Aneksi wiped the tears from the edge of her eyes, shaking her head.

"No, no...I speak the truth...my baby..."

Her vision darkened, and she saw the shadow of a large bird fly above her.

Aneksi lifted her wrist, seeing her bracelet was not on her. Her blood stilled. When had she taken it off?

"Your Highness, speak louder."

Aneksi opened her mouth, but another jolt of pain ran through her body and she dropped to the floor with a scream.

Kiya took a fearful step away from her while guards rushed to their fallen queen. The scribes glanced at one another, hesitating to record what was happening.

The Pharaoh, this time, tore away the curtain and rushed down the steps in an attempt to reach Aneksi. His personal guards stopped him from getting any farther than a few meters away from her hunched form.

"Your Greatness, if Her Highness has an illness, You mustn't go near her," one of them said.

Aneksi was lifted out of the chamber, too succumbed to the pain to even walk.

"You are all dismissed," the Pharaoh said, glancing at Kiya, indicating that the trial would be rescheduled. She bowed her head and exited, followed by the scribes.

The Pharaoh shut his eyes as the viziers, Kenbets, and the High Priest of Horus stepped out from behind the curtain. Kahorus had been the only High Priest nearest to the Palace at the time the Pharaoh had called for a trial, and so was asked to be part of the judging panel.

"It must be difficult to see, but she swore an oath to speak by Ma'at and yet she was struck down as she spoke," the High Priest said.

"No," the Pharaoh shot back, his voice strong but shaken.

"What else is there to assume?" Kahorus continued. He turned his stout body to look at the viziers and Kenbets, who kept silent with furrowed brows in thought. "If my presumption is wrong, please give me another explanation. We have little proof to defend Her Highness, don't we? I'm sorry, I can only declare her guilty."

One or two viziers mumbled an agreement. The Kenbets frowned.

"We should put forth an investigation. We know too little," one said. Kahorus scoffed.

A vizier who agreed with High Priest nodded at his disapproval.

"There have been too many questionable actions regarding Her Highness. Who is to say her kidnapping was not staged to remove the poison's trace from the Palace?"

The Pharaoh's eyes flashed in anger at this. "How dare you assume this?" he shouted. "Neferkempi was shaken after that ordeal! I lost a good servant in trying to rescue her!"

"Perhaps he was killed by her or her supporters when he realized the truth of her leaving?" Kahorus prompted. The Pharaoh stared, wide-eyed.

"Then what of the other guard? Why spare him?"

Kahorus shrugged. "I have seen the way he regards Her Highness. He could very well be a part of it."

Exhaling, the Pharaoh shook his head.

"This is far too much, Kahorus."

The High Priest bowed his head. When he lifted his face up, the shadows of the fire obscured most of his face.

"I only seek the best for my King and his succession."

The Pharaoh grunted, glancing wearily at the High Priest. "Thank you for your council tonight. You must all stay the night. We'll resume this tomorrow."

The Kenbets nodded, as did Kahorus.

As the men filed out of the chamber, the Pharaoh clasped his arm around Kahorus', stopping him. Standing a foot taller, the Pharaoh loomed over the wide High Priest.

"I warn you, Kahorus. Do not be so antagonistic to my wife," the Pharaoh said in a low voice. "It won't benefit the tardiness of your taxes."

Kahorus swallowed hard. "Of course."

The Pharaoh let go of the High Priest and gave him a solemn nod.

"Sleep well, Kahorus."

PART XXIII.

"Has the bleeding stopped?"

It was dawn; and the distant, rising red sun illuminated the chamber and skies, as if Ra himself had painted the blood of his child across the land.

Aneksi's eyes were half-open, for she had dreaded sleep without her father's charm as she lay on the bed in the surgical hall. She was in nothing but her undergarments, her face devoid of any of its powder. Her legs were parted, and at the foot of the bed was a basket of dark ruby-hued cloth that hid the carcass of what should have been.

"Yes," the physician said in a low voice. He was young, perhaps as old as Meryt, with the somber gaze of an antelope. Neither the High Priest nor his granddaughter was in the Palace, leaving such royal matters to Nekure, Ekmati's apprentice and son of the Pharaoh's half-sister, Epehshert. "You do understand what this means, Your Highness."

Aneksi closed her eyes fully this time and let her tears trickle down her face. Her sobs were met with silence. Nekure sighed lightly to express his sympathy for her, and rinsed Aneksi's legs and abdomen with warm water, trying to massage away the only pains he could from her.

Just as Nekure stepped forward to wipe her face of her tears, he felt a hand on his shoulder to stop him. Nekure took a quick step away from Aneksi and knelt.

"Your Greatness, Uncle."

The Pharaoh gave him a small smile at his quick recognition. He was wearing armor that belonged to one of his personal guards. Being that most of the servants in the Palace did not directly deal with the Pharaoh, with just an outfit change he could roam the halls unaware of his identity and therefore no one to call him out for breaking the law.

The Pharaoh bent down to run his fingers down Aneksi's cheek. Seeing her lying in such a state reminded how fragile his happiness was; without Aneksi steadfast in life, the Pharaoh knew he could only imagine a life of constant mourning.

"By the gods, what happened to you?" he whispered.

At the sound of his voice, Aneksi's eyes fluttered open, her heart beating wildly at his touch. With eyes now open, Aneksi let out a muffled moan, fresh tears springing in her eyes.

"F-forgive me."

"Neferkempi-"

"I took away our son," she continued, choking out the words. The Pharaoh inhaled sharply, and his eyes trailed to the gruesome sight at the foot of the bed. He glanced at Nekure and the physician nodded solemnly.

The Pharaoh turned to face Aneksi and softly placed his lips on her brow. "There is no reason for you to mourn so, Neferkempi. You've done no wrong."

Aneksi gripped the Pharaoh's wrists, staring up at him with wide eyes. She could not understand the sound of hope and love in his words.

"I have disappointed you by not having carried your child to birth. And I have disgraced my father by bringing these allegations to our family. I have proven only to be a failure. How can I ever think to stay by you?" she whispered. "How can I think to lift my head again?"

"No, no," the Pharaoh shook his head, pressing his forehead to hers. "You mustn't give up on me. I promised to you keep you at my side, Neferkempi. And I swear by the gods, nothing will change that. Do you understand?"

Aneksi nodded a fraction. The Pharaoh gave her an encouraging smile, wiping away her tears.

"I ask that you fear nothing regarding your trial. It will be over soon. My only wish for you is to recover, quickly, for both our sake." The Pharaoh turned his head and spoke over his shoulder to address Nekure. "No one is to know I visited here. And prepare my child for his funeral."

The unborn child was taken to be buried in private.

Aneksi spent the rest of the day at the surgical hall, recovering. Nekure, exempted from the no contact rule due to her condition, kept Aneksi company.

"I've always admired Lady Meryt," Nekure had told her. "I have seen her precision with a blade in the surgical halls and when preparing the dead." Aneksi only half listened, but just the sound of someone speaking to her soothed a part of her heart. "She keeps such detailed records and the High Priest often lets her do most of the tonic creating. Perhaps one day Uncle will recognize her prowess and have her take after the High Priest."

Rai helped prepare her meals, mainly consisting of Acacia to stop the bleeding. He also brought good news by noon: The Pharaoh had promised a verdict by nightfall after another undecided hearing earlier in the morning.

She knew not to worry. Only overcome the scars of what had happened. Aneski felt better simply thinking about the Pharaoh's promise of life returning to normal. But still, until she could contact her father about a replacement charm, Aneksi only allowed herself short naps and the soothing herbal drinks made from honey and poppy seeds that Nekure offered to make up for her lack of sleep.

While she rested, Nekure read over Meryt's notes on Aneksi's pregnancy and later concluded it with his own.

Aneksi did not see Lithra at all that day, but she was too preoccupied with the flashing pains in her abdomen and lack of sleep to take notice.

When night had fallen, Aneksi was called to the throne

room as promised. The screen was once again up to conceal the identities of the Great Kenbet, but only the Pharaoh sat unhidden upon his throne.

Kiya, her guards, and the scribes were also there, awaiting their decision. Aneksi stood with Rai's aid, holding onto his outstretched forearm to remain upright. Upon seeing her condition, Kiya glanced Aneski's way a few times, her expression a mix of confusion and distrust.

After all had come, the Pharaoh raised his hand to quiet the room and spoke.

"Since nothing conclusive could be drawn between Lady Aneksi and the poisoning, it has been decided that Lady Aneksi is innocent of the allegations put forth. The testimony of a criminal is not strong enough to convict."

Kiya was unable to hide her shock, her jaw dropping. Aneksi felt her chest swell as the Pharaoh made eye contact with her, almost as if he were conveying his happiness through his eyes.

"She will be excluded in any private events regarding Ankhetep and Ka-Rae, but only temporarily," the Pharaoh continued. "A month was the original mandate; however, my son refused such an extensive time and, in this regard, I have concluded that Lady Aneksi will be sentenced only a week."

Kiya turned her head away at the Pharaoh's words, wrinkling her nose, while Aneksi's eyes widened. Neither women had expected the Pharaoh would take into consideration what Ankhetep thought of the accusations.

Rising from his seat, the Pharaoh outstretched his arms. "This is decision has been made by the will of the gods, and so it shall be."

Kiya and Aneksi bowed their heads at the decision as the scribes drew the last of the trial on paper.

After all were dismissed, the Pharaoh walked Aneksi back to their private chamber. It felt somewhat strange to Aneksi as she settled down beside him. Everything had changed so fast for her, yet here she was at his side again, as if all were well. There was a sense of foreignness, but at the same time, it was relaxing to see the curtained doorway to their private garden swaying in the breeze and hearing the gentle hiss and pop of the candles above them.

The Pharaoh spent most of their time awake speaking about general affairs.

"I received a letter notifying that the remaining priests from the Lower Lands will arrive in two and a half weeks. A dust storm stopped them from joining the others earlier. I hope you will have recovered your strength by then to participate in the coronation," he said. Aneksi nodded. The Pharaoh continued after a small pause. "Some of the harvests have come in smaller and with more complaints from the tax collectors. I sent guards to make sure nothing was being stolen by thieves, but that meant the extra guards I assigned on your behalf was reduced." He quickly added, "After all, it has been quite some time since...then and I have been given no reports of suspicious activity."

Aneksi placed her hand on the Pharaoh's chest. She had thought to speak about Ahset and Akhara's plea deal regarding their harvests but realized this was not the issue the Pharaoh was concerned over.

"You're right to make such a call. It would seem rather a waste to keep those guards expecting a threat that may very well have fled the Palace with no intention of returning."

The Pharaoh smiled. "Yes, I do think that's the case. There's also been some unrest in a market town just beyond us. I expect a visit from the Great Royal Wife will keep them in good thoughts."

"Oh?" Aneksi propped herself up, staring at the Pharaoh. "You know I'm not well versed on how to deal with such issues," she said with a frown. The Pharaoh chuckled and leaned forward to kiss her bare shoulder.

"Indeed. But I do know you are capable if pressed into the situation. I won't be able to accompany you when you are there, as they are upset regarding a hunting tax I implemented, but I'll make sure you are acquainted with their regional priests to understand and address their concerns properly." Aneksi nodded at this, though she still felt light-headed at the thought of her doing something beyond what she knew. "Now, let's sleep," the Pharaoh said.

Aneksi settled into the Pharaoh's embrace and closed her eyes only briefly. She felt him kiss her head and sigh into her neck. Aneksi could not bring herself to smile at his relief but pressed against him with the hope that the night would end on this happy note.

PART XXIV.

In the days that followed, Aneksi could sometimes hear a rush of little reed sandals run up to her consort chamber door before hearing it angrily stomp away. She smiled at the thought of Ankhetep so anxious for her sentence to be over and his desire to be with her eased the pain in her chest from losing her own child.

In this time Aneksi was also allowed to contact her father. He was extremely distraught at both the loss of his first charm and more so of the child. Unable to leave his duties with the beginning of the tax collections, he could do nothing more except have her charm replaced.

On the seventh morning, before either the Pharaoh or Aneksi could even wake up, Ankhetep burst in through the door to their private chamber, shouting, "I can see Her Highness again!" over and over as he scrambled to climb up their bed.

The Pharaoh grunted as Ankhetep sat between the two. Aneksi slowly rose to sit up, wiping her eyes to look down at the jittery boy.

"How is my sibling-to-come?" he asked. Aneksi froze, blinking at Ankhetep for a moment before her gaze slid to meet the Pharaoh's. His eyes had shot open at Ankhetep's question. "Mother has given me a brother and I only await the news of yours."

Neither knew how to tell him the child was gone.

Ankhetep, before either monarch could say anything, pressed his ear to Aneksi's stomach. She swallowed hard, her throat dry. The Pharaoh propped himself up on his elbow and gently brought Ankhetep away from Aneksi.

Just as he did so, Ankhetep said, "I can hear it!"

"What?" Aneksi shared a wide-eyed look with the

Pharaoh.

"I'll rephrase: I can hear the heartbeat as you once showed me how," he said. Ankhetep pulled on the Pharaoh's hand playfully, smiling at the two.

"That's not..." Aneksi began before her voice trailed off.

"Ankhetep," the Pharaoh said, making the boy look directly at him, "does the heartbeat you hear sound like mine?" The boy leaned over and pressed an ear to the Pharaoh's chest, his eyes narrowed, and lips pursed in concentration.

After a moment, Ankhetep pulled away.

"Yes, it does sound similar."

Hearing him, Aneksi brought her hand over her mouth, her eyes watering. How was it possible?

"Ankhetep, I'd like for you to wait outside and seek out permission to enter next time," the Pharaoh said, distracting the boy from seeing Aneksi. "Do that now." With a frown, Ankhetep did as told, hopping off the bed. He slipped on his sandals and left the chamber.

Once gone, the Pharaoh immediately turned to Aneksi, pulling her by the waist to sit closer to him. Over his shoulder, he called out to one of his personal guards.

The guard appeared and knelt at the doorway.

"Bring the High Priest of Sekhmet at once," he said. "If not him, then his granddaughter or apprentice. Anyone competent."

After the guard had left, Aneksi placed a hand on the Pharaoh's arm.

"Can you hear it too?" she whispered.

The Pharaoh hesitated but shifted his ear to place it upon her abdomen. Aneksi shut her eyes. She prayed Ankhetep was not mistaken. The Pharaoh moved back and Aneksi opened her eyes to look at him. She held her breath, waiting for his confirmation.

Meryt rushed inside, capturing Aneksi and the Pharaoh's attention. He sat up and put an arm around Aneksi's waist to indicate her as he spoke.

"The child was lost some nights ago, but there is still an audible heartbeat. How can this be?" he asked.

Meryt gripped the scroll in her hand.

"I suspected Her Highness to have a double pregnancy," she said in a firm voice. Aneksi bent over, placing a hand over her chest. Twins? The Pharaoh stared, open-mouthed as Meryt added, "If only one child was lost as Nekure has written, then..."

"One is still alive," the Pharaoh finished. Meryt gave a

curt nod. The Pharaoh gave Aneksi a tight squeeze, shaking his head. He turned his head to look at Meryt again. "Why did the apprentice not inform us of this?"

"I was unsure of my finding as we have never predicted a double pregnancy before. Nekure must have not wanted to bring misinformation during such a delicate time."

"Our child is still alive?" Aneksi whispered, her hand traveling to her abdomen. Her eyes found the Pharaoh's and she pressed her forehead to his shoulder, and began to cry.

"Shh," the Pharaoh murmured, stroking her back. Though with his own eyes glistening, he said, "How can we cry at such wonderful news?"

Meryt bowed her head and silently exited the chamber.

Aneksi was looking herself over in her consort chamber when Lithra ran in. Aneksi was dressed in a silver fitted gown, a single slit running down from her thigh to her ankle. She wore steel wristlets and two thin golden bands around her left arm.

Lithra halted before Aneksi, breathing hard. The bandages were still around her chest, waist, and legs, but it seemed she had no trouble moving about.

"Is it true?" Lithra whispered. "Is it true that you're still pregnant?"

Aneksi turned away from the mirror, folding her two hands over the protruding bump. She smiled down at her slave, tears forming in her eyes again.

"Yes. Yes, it is."

Lithra dropped to her knees, wailing.

"Oh, gods! Oh, gods!" she cried.

Aneksi shifted back, slightly shocked by Lithra's reaction. Shaking her head, Aneksi slowly sank to the floor to place a hand on Lithra's shoulder. The girl looked up, tears streaming down her cheeks.

"Does this news truly bring this much happiness to you?" Aneksi asked with a small smile. "I would've-"

"Happy?" Lithra hissed, pulling away from Aneksi's hand. "Does this look like happiness to you? I'm in anguish! In pain! In misery! I wanted your baby dead!"

Aneksi recoiled at her last words, falling onto the cold floor. She shook with shock and fear.

"What did you say?" Aneksi breathed, her eyes wide.

Lithra's blue eyes were rimmed with burst blood vessels. Her right hand slowly withdrew a jagged chunk of ceramic, perhaps from a broken jar, from the cotton sash about her waist. She gripped it tightly, her jaws clenched.

"I cannot trust anything but myself to get this done. Slaves hesitate to obey, and poison can miss its target. Only I must end the life unworthy soul in your womb."

"But you forgave me for having your hand–"

"Silence! You and your father have ruined my life far more than just cutting my hand!" Lithra dove for Aneksi with a scream, the clay shard poised to tear away flesh.

Aneksi shrieked and kicked out wildly, one foot coming in contact with Lithra's chest and the other her chin, sending Lithra backward. Fumbling back along the stone floor, Aneksi called out to the guards, throwing floor cushions and sofa pillows in Lithra's direction to slow down her recovery from the kicks.

When no one rushed to the sound of her call, Aneksi brought herself up and ran for the door. Lithra stood up slowly, breathing loudly as she watched Aneksi with narrowed blue eyes. Aneksi stumbled into Rai when she pushed open the door. He shook his head and blinked down at her.

"Your High–?"

"She is trying to kill my child!" Aneksi nearly shouted, gripping onto his chest plate. Rai straightened, his arm shifting to hover around her waist, and glanced about.

"Who?"

"Lithra! She said so herself! She wanted to kill my second child!"

"Is she in your chamber?" Aneksi nodded mutely. "Stay behind me," Rai instructed as he slowly made his way inside.

The chamber looked as if nothing had been ajar. Aneksi's mouth fell open, seeing the pillows back where they were. Lithra was nowhere to be seen.

"Are you sure she was here?" Rai asked, turning back to face Aneksi.

"Of course. Did you not hear me call out for you?"

Rai frowned, a hand over his chin in thought. "I didn't."

Aneksi closed her eyes briefly. She placed her hands over her face, shaking her head. What was going on? For what reason would Lithra bear so much hate for her? 'You and your father' she had said. What had they done?

PART XXV.

Aneksi was forced to leave the incident that had just occurred behind her. She was to make a public appearance on the Pharaoh's behalf soon and was told she needed to participate in a meeting to learn how to speak and deal with the matter; and with no proof of Lithra's acts or any trace of her in the Palace, Aneksi could not ask for anything to be done against her.

The townspeople were in awe of Aneksi's presence. After stepping down from the palanquin, she forced a smile at those who had gathered around. They bowed, and some knelt on the sandy, cracked earth. Many were wearing worn tunics and dresses, faded and patched.

Aneksi was taken inside the town's only Temple. Because the town was often a pit stop for traders from all over on their way to the Palace, the number of gods the priests maintained numbered over twenty. Carved statues of all sizes and all material types –clay, limestone, even obsidian– lined the walls. The floors were painted in various colors with no distinct pattern. Incenses with great fragrances burned, giving the air a sweet taste. A single altar was placed at the front of the Temple, but there was no statue or depiction of a patron god or goddess.

Aneksi was given the wooden seat at the altar while the priests sat on the floor. Rai was the only guard who had entered, while the rest had taken positions around the Temple. A table was set beside her with wine and a variety of fruits and cooked meats in silver platters.

"I was told the people are restless," Aneksi said, frowning lightly. "As the men who carry out your Pharaoh's decree, I am disappointed in you all."

The priests bowed their heads. Their leader, wearing a golden cotton-spun robe, spoke.

"Please forgive us, Your Highness!" he said. "The people have refused to pay the last few weeks."

Aneksi's frown deepened and thought back to her lesson earlier in the day regarding her options. She could send Palace guards during the tax collection to help the priests persuade the people. But seeing as they had been so shocked at her arrival, perhaps scaring them would be the wrong impression. Aneksi looked back down at the priest.

"Is there anything you suggest we do? You know these people better than I do."

The lead priest looked at the others before clearing his throat. "Perhaps...a tax increase?"

"How would that help?" Aneksi asked, cocking her head. "Aren't they refusing to comply because it's too much to pay?"

"Ah no," he quickly said. "I feel that they see this tax as excusable seeing as it's such a minuscule amount that's being asked of them." Aneksi glanced at Rai. His eyebrows were knitted as he watched the priest speak. She had never heard of such a thing. "If we raise the tax to half, instead of a tenth, of what they hunt, the people will submit."

"Half?" Aneksi sat back. Not even her father had ever taxed so high and he still had many disputes to quell. "That seems quite outrageous."

"Of course," the lead priest bowed his head again. "I say this only for His Majesty's sake. How can we serve Him as his servants when we have so little to offer? I am deeply ashamed."

"I see." Aneksi gave him a strained smile.

"Your Highness, please have something to eat!" the priest beside the head priest said, indicating to the table next to her. "This decision can wait, as your health is far superior!"

Aneksi shook her head, a hand absently over her stomach as she glanced at the food on the table. She would be wise to take better care of the child she still had.

"I will pass," she said. "But thank you."

"Do not thank us, Your Highness!" the other priest said. "You are worth a thousand lives!"

Aneksi smiled at the words, nodding her head a little. She motioned for Rai to approach.

"Is it allowed of me to ask the people how to fix this?" she whispered.

Rai shook his head. "It's not something the Royals or priests do."

"May I still?" Aneksi asked. "I feel that what the priests have suggested is something the Pharaoh would not give his approval for. And I have no better an idea to resolve this. Perhaps they have a compromise to suggest in all this." Rai nodded solemnly.

Aneksi turned to face the priests once more. They had begun eating already. Seeing her attention on them, they dropped their plates.

"It's alright, please remain as you are. I simply wish to see the town a bit before I come to a conclusion." The priests bowed their heads.

Rai guided her down the altar and Aneksi set forth into the town.

The peasant children ran into their homes upon seeing Aneksi walk along their street. She wrinkled her nose at the burning smell in the air, feeling her stomach twist. Just what were they cooking?

"Rai, what is that horrid smell? Tell them to stop," Aneksi said, covering her mouth with the back of her hand. She held back a gag. Rai nodded and went up to each of the homes to request what Aneksi had asked of them.

When he returned, much of the smell had gone.

"Thank you," Aneksi said. "What were they burning?"

Rai looked away.

"Mice and dog meat, Your Highness."

Aneksi felt her stomach shift at the thought. She swallowed hard.

"But if a hunting tax was placed here, why are they eating such things? Should they not be eating fowl or the meat of what they are catching?"

Rai stared hard in the distance. "That would be expected, yes."

Aneksi looked at the peering children from their homes. They quickly hid.

"I'd like to consult the Pharaoh," she said, a hand on her temple. "None of this makes any sense to me. Tell the priests I'm leaving now."

Rai bowed and motioned for the other guards to take their position alongside the palanquin before sending another to let the priests know.

By the time the priests stepped out, bellies full, Aneksi was settled in her seat and did not wish to accept their personal farewells. Once at the Palace, Aneksi ate her nightly meal. The Pharaoh had been busing dealing with a construction affair for the past few days and Aneksi did not want to interfere.

In bed, when the two had settled in, the Pharaoh asked of her outing.

"Were you able to reach a solution?" the Pharaoh said.

"No, I was not," Aneksi said with a frown.

"Oh? What trouble did you find then?"

Aneksi sighed. "The priests asked for a tax hike." The Pharaoh raised an eyebrow. "I refused knowing it would be too much. Those townspeople eat mice of all things! How could I agree?"

"Mice? Are you sure?" the Pharaoh asked, frowning.

"I couldn't stand the smell," Aneksi affirmed. The Pharaoh pursed his lips.

"How can that be? My viziers told me a flock or two of geese and a herd of antelope had begun migrating along their hunting grounds because of a brushfire in their previous home. Mice are the last these people should be eating in a land so blessed."

"The priests seemed to have eaten well," Aneksi mumbled. The Pharaoh turned to her as she continued. "They had their plates full."

"Did they?" Aneksi nodded. The Pharaoh exhaled in disbelief. "They swore to me that the townspeople refused to give their taxes and in result, they were starving. My vizier allowed them to keep half of what they had when it was time to collect the tax. Those lying wretches!" the Pharaoh shook his head in disgust. He turned his gaze to her. "You did well not to have heeded their advice and seek my counsel. I'll have someone finish this for you. Such dastardly men have no right to be blessed by your presence."

Aneksi smiled; she was pleased to know that she had acted properly on her first political affair. The Pharaoh leaned over and kissed her stomach. He locked her eyes with his.

"But enough of this business. You need your rest, Neferkempi. I pray to the gods all will be well for this child's birth."

PART XXVI.

Aneksi bathed in a separate, private pool because of her pregnancy; and while it was a comforting gesture from the Pharaoh, it only isolated her more. Kiya withheld Ankhetep from visiting and Meryt had only just returned with her grandfather and the two were busy fixing a mishap in the storage and records halls. And with the coronation only days away, the Pharaoh spent most of his time speaking with priests from the Lower Lands, his viziers, and many of the wealthy merchants for their favor, support, and coordination for the event.

It left Aneski to delve into her own thoughts about Lithra's treacherous acts. Aneksi could not worry her father nor the Pharaoh about this, and so decided she needed to deal with Lithra before she disrupted the coronation and public announcement of her pregnancy. Aneksi was left with no option but to put herself in a position where Lithra would to come to her rather than continue the fruitless search for her ex-slave.

Aneksi was kneeling at the foot of Ma'at's statue.

The stars above her winked and glittered, but the only light came from inside the private chamber where the Pharaoh slept. Rai was hidden in the shadows of a nearby obelisk, his eyes closed, and ears trained for movement.

A cold breeze swept through the garden, rustling the leaves.

"Have you given up looking for me? Is that why you wait here so obediently?" Aneksi looked up, searching the dark still air for Lithra. But her eyes came up short. "You wish to know why I have done this, yes? Of course you do, Ani; you are easier to read than any book."

Aneksi stood up, turning around to press her back against

Ma'at.

"Come forward, Lithra. We end this tonight."

The girl stepped out from the shadows, her blue eyes cold. She stepped between the entrance to the private chamber and Aneksi, swallowing what little light there was. Lithra wore a half-dress, exposing her non-bandaged arms and legs. Around her neck she wore a pendant, but it was too dark for Aneksi to see what it exactly was.

"How could you do this to me, after all the years we spent together?" Aneksi asked in disbelief. "You were treated so well, by my mother and myself-"

Lithra's hand curled into a fist.

"Is that how you saw it? Of course, you would. Ani, you were always so blind. My nightmares first started when your father forced himself upon me."

Aneksi gasped, a hand to her chest. "No...you're lying! My father would never do such a thing!"

"I lived in that monster's home, always afraid and reminded of your blissful ignorance. And then you forced me to take your place when the Pharaoh came to court you." Lithra let out an angry sigh. "Who knew a slave could fall in love? And think they had any chance of fulfilling it?"

"What?" Aneksi's hand drifted to her side. "You fell in

love with the Pharaoh?"

"Yes!" Lithra shouted, her blue eyes bright with tears. "You forced me into loving him. For months, he kept coming back. I swore it was because of his love for me! He was awed by my intellect, and oh, how he praised my beauty. And then you ripped him away from me even though you assured me that you loved another."

"Lithra I–"

"When the Pharaoh came for you, it was as if my body was stolen from me again. But it was not your father who did it this time. It was you."

Aneksi shook her head, bile rising in her throat. Was this why Lithra had become so cold after her marriage?

"The child you bear does not belong to you." Lithra's voice had gone hard and the tears that had slipped from her eyes were now gone. "It should belong to me."

"But Lithra this is absurd!" Aneksi frantically said, blinking furiously. "How–? How could I have–?"

Lithra took a single step closer, making Aneksi press back against the cold statue.

"This should be a fair warning to you, Ani. I am not the only one who likes to see you suffer." She smiled at the creeping fear in Aneksi's face. "The gods' favor can change as easily as the night air does. I may have been your dutiful slave once, but I no longer answer to you. Nor do I wish to see you alive any longer." Lithra produced a dagger from her back and threw it at her.

Rai jumped from his position, using his spear divert the dagger's direction. It clattered onto the ground by the foot of another obelisk. Using his body as a shield to cover Aneksi, Rai looked over his shoulder only to see that Lithra was gone.

He turned back to Aneksi. "Are you alright, Your Highness?"

Aneksi was gripping her arms, shaking, her eyes glazed over with shock and disbelief at everything that had unfolded.

"I..." Aneksi blinked rapidly. She glanced up at Rai, her eyes too dark to make out. "I don't understand...."

"You have everything you asked for," Rai said, stepping back. "What will you do now, Your Highness?"

Aneksi sighed, pressing a fist to her forehead in despair.

"I have no idea. Should I finally tell the Pharaoh about this?"

Rai furrowed his eyebrows in thought. "Lithra is most certainly a suspect to the events that have plagued your stay here. She may have confessed to it, but there is no other evidence besides that. A trial on her behalf would return questionable, especially seeing how elusive she has been. It might even be impossible for us to have her on trial in person."

Aneksi let out a small whimper, her eyes watering.

"You're right. The Pharaoh said nothing was found regarding the people who tried to kill me."

"What I can suggest is to watch for any of Lithra's movements. She said others shared in her anger so there is a great chance they are aiding each other. Although it may be difficult to capture Lithra, her accomplices may not be so careful and slip up. We simply need more time and clues to put everything together."

Aneksi pressed her hands against the marble statue as Rai spoke. Ma'at help them. It would not be easy.

Aneksi returned to the Pharaoh's side and watched him sleep for several moments. She ran her fingers along his temple down to his jaw. The candlelight flickered along his face, brightening his bronze complexion to that of one mixed with molten gold. Closing her eyes, Aneksi pressed herself against him, tears falling silently down her cheeks. The coronation would only increase Lithra's disdain. But she could not back down from it. Perhaps it would lure her and the 'others' she referenced out of hiding.

After a minute or two, Aneksi opened her eyes and glanced down at the bump in her stomach. What a perilous world she was bringing her child into.

PART XXVII.

"Rise, O Great Royal Wife, Queen of the Nile."

Aneksi stood up and turned to face the crowd of priests, noblemen, and the extended Royal Family. The sun's rays ran through the turquoise sheer cape stretching from below her mid-back to the floor, making the air shimmer around her. A solid gold girdle pinched her waist, her forearms covered in gilded armor, and her neck showered by beads of gold and turquoise. The wind billowed against the light cotton dress along her body and the tall modius atop her head shifted as she surveyed the tipped heads before her. The upper half of Aneksi's face was painted with crushed jewels and outlined in powdered lead, weighing heavily against her eyes.

Aneksi could barely contain herself before the crowd; she was now the Blackland's -not just the Pharaoh's- Great Royal Wife. And soon-to-be mother of the Pharaoh's next child.

"Kneel before Her Royal Highness."

The crowds did as ordered, except the five women sitting atop the shoulders of their guards. Instead, the Pharaoh's consorts bowed their heads. Ahset and Akhara were the last to do so, scowling to show their open disapproval. But Aneksi's gaze did not linger on them.

The coronation was taking place in the Tri-God Temple, with her father initiating it. Tears sprung in Aneksi's eyes as her gaze settled from column to column. She had brought great honor to her ancestors. Aneksi placed her hands briefly over her growing belly. And she would be passing down their legacy for those who would come after her.

"May she reign with a thousand blessings, and the child she carries exalted to the gods." With that finishing line, Aneksi slowly made her way down the steps.

A breeze blew by as she did so, scattering the flower petals at the base of the temple. The crowd parted as she neared to allow her a pathway. Waiting for her at the center of the spectators was the Pharaoh's palanquin, where he had watched her accept her title as Queen.

The Pharaoh was lowered enough to hold out his hand for Aneksi. They would ride through the city together as King and Queen before returning for a celebratory banquet.

As Aneksi neared him, the consorts were lowered to the ground. Meryt flashed her a small smile. Ahset and Akhara clenched their jaw and looked away. Kiya remained as she was, sitting tall with a nonchalant expression. Khemut kept her head bowed.

Aneksi took his hand and was lifted to sit down beside the Pharaoh. She settled in with a sigh.

"You're not too fatigued this morning, are you?" the Pharaoh asked as she leaned into his shoulder.

"No, not too much today," Aneksi whispered.

The two were jostled a bit as they were lifted into the air, but the Pharaoh held tightly onto Aneksi's hand and used his free one to run his thumb back and forth along her thigh to ease her anxiousness.

"I prepared for us to visit Ahmose," the Pharaoh said after a time. He watched Neferkempi close her eyes at the name, her lips quivering.

Ahmose.

It was the name the Pharaoh had chosen for their miscarried child before his life had come to an abrupt end. The Pharaoh exhaled his grief, bringing a hand to her cheek. She caught his hand, the other over her abdomen. Neither had much time to grieve over the loss because of the coronation.

"Our son is with the gods, as he should be," the Pharaoh assured her. He had to stay strong for her. What else could he do?

"I wanted him here, with us," she whispered, her eyes threatening to ruin the hours spent to perfect her face.

The Pharaoh squeezed her hand.

"The gods know we do," he said, pressing his forehead to hers. "That's why we have this second chance now." Neferkempi inhaled deeply and nodded. But the Pharaoh knew his words could only mean so much.

Ribbons and flowers were tossed around their palanquin as the royal couple passed through the towns. Six horsemen and ten armed footmen flanked them. Afterward, they were taken to the Royal Tomb where Ahmose had been properly mummified and buried in a coffin of his own.

The Royal Tombs were north of the Palace and built underground. Aneksi was led down a flight of steps, with the only light coming from the torch in Rai's hand. The air was damp and dusty in the stairwell, but it cleared up once they entered the central chambers.

In the hall meant for the Pharaoh's family, beside the empty coffin where the Pharaoh would be laid to rest, was the coffin that belonged to Ahmose. It was a mere seven inches long, just slightly larger than one's hand. The stone was painted and carved as ornately as any of his predecessors' coffins were.

The Pharaoh held Aneksi as she sobbed into his chest. His own tears had fallen, streaming down his cheeks. The Pharaoh clung to her and felt her abdomen press into him. He would never forgive himself should anything happen to either of them.

When they returned to the Palace, the two composed themselves and even called servants to wash and repaint their faces to appear as if they had never grieved.

The Throne Room had been altered for the ceremonial banquet, as it was the only chamber large enough to house all the guests for such a momentous occasion. The Royal family and the priests were given a higher table to eat upon than the rest of the noblemen, wealthy merchants, and their families. A dozen or so servants ran about, filling cups and re-plating food. Palace guards stood along the walls and doorway, along with the personal guards the priests from the Lower Lands had brought with them.

As a Palace servant came by to serve Aneksi, the Pharaoh was struck by a thought.

"Neferkempi, where is that slave of yours, Lithra?" he asked. Aneksi stiffened in her seat. "I've seen her run about here and there in the Palace, but she is never by your side these days."

"There's been some issues in her regard," Aneksi answered slowly.

"Have you released her from your ownership, then?"

Aneksi turned to face the Pharaoh with a frown. "No...Lithra has been insubordinate of late. I would have called her to trial for her actions but there has been no time to bring it up to you."

"Insubordinate?" he repeated, raising his eyebrows. "If that's so, you wouldn't need my permission to have her sent away."

Aneksi briefly closed her eyes while the Pharaoh lifted his cup to his lips to drink. She lowered her voice, noticing that several of the priests from the Lower Lands had turned to watch them.

"Her actions are more than just that...they are treasonous. She confessed to wanting our child dead."

The Pharaoh coughed, setting his cup down to stare at Aneksi with wide eyes.

"What?"

Aneksi looked away.

"I wouldn't have believed it had I not been the witness to her confession."

The Pharaoh sighed, shaking his head. How could this be? He knew Lithra to be quite smart and amicable. How could she want such a thing?

"I am glad we can finally confront it now, as things will return to normal after a day or two," the Pharaoh finally said, forcing a smile as he turned to look at the court of guests before them. News of this would be disastrous so soon after the coronation. He turned his head briefly back to Aneksi. "There's much we will have to do."

PART XXVIII.

Aneksi's father was called to meet with the Pharaoh after the guests had left from the coronation ceremony the following morning. He, the Pharaoh, and Aneksi were seated in the portico, faces grim. The curtains to the window had been drawn shut, leaving the sconces along the walls as the only source of light. No servants were present in the chamber.

Kairunamete was sitting beside Aneksi in the low cushions while the Pharaoh sat opposite of them.

Aneksi sighed. "This all began when Lithra started acting strangely once we came to the Palace."

"I would like to know why this is being brought up now," her father interrupted with a frown.

"How could I worry any of you over her?" Aneksi glanced to the Pharaoh and back to her father. Her hand went to touch the charm bracelet she still wore. "There was so much going on, I didn't think much of it."

Kairunamete pressed his lips in a firm line, dissatisfied. He sat back with his arms folded across his chest and eyes closed in deep thought.

"You told me she confessed," the Pharaoh said, drawing her attention. "What exactly did she say?" Aneksi swallowed hard.

"She said she had wanted our child gone, that I was unworthy of it." Aneksi paused, then her eyes widened.

"Neferkempi?" the Pharaoh asked, leaning forward a bit.

"The morning we found out I was still pregnant, Lithra said 'poison can miss.' She served me food and drink right before the trial. Perhaps it was not stress that had caused Ahmose to leave us. What if...?"

"Dear gods," the Pharaoh whispered, face paling.

Kairunamete opened his eyes.

"Was this slave of yours also with you when you were kidnapped from the Palace?" he asked, his voice low.

Aneksi turned to fully face her father. "Yes. But you don't think-?"

"It could very well be so," he cut her off.

"He makes a valid assumption, Neferkempi; and now that I think of it, it does make sense." The Pharaoh ran a hand over his face, eyebrows furrowed. "The guards who escorted you out of the Palace were found dead, including the two women at the establishment you were taken to, and an unidentified boy. The only other person alive regarding the incident is she." The Pharaoh exhaled loudly. "But what could possibly turn her against you? I never saw her as vengeful before this."

Aneksi blinked furiously. Her mind raced to think of some way to not tell them that Lithra falling in love with the Pharaoh was the reason behind it all. Not only that, how could she accuse her own father of lewdness on Lithra's allegation alone?

"She told me she was not the only one who wanted me dead," Aneksi managed to say.

"Of course there is someone in the Palace helping her," Kairunamete frowned again. "A mere slave has no will to do such acts unless there is power driving them." The Pharaoh narrowed his eyes as Kairunamete spoke on. "I do have an inkling of who it could possibly be, but there isn't enough proof to lay blame. Aneksi, did your slave show any compassion for any of the other consorts?"

Aneksi glanced at the Pharaoh and met his gaze. His eyes had softened, and she knew if she linked any of his other wives to this it would pain him. Aneksi forced herself to look away and let out a sigh.

"I had Lithra's hand cut off," she began. Both her father and the Pharaoh's eyes widened at the statement. "It was a punishment: She struck me across the face when I refused to accept Lady Ahset and Lady Akhara's offer to deny being Queen, so they could help the villages loyal to them."

"Kahorus did mention a drought in some of his lands," the Pharaoh finally said in a low voice. "But I don't know how severe."

A silence followed.

"Horus, the god of the sky; He who exacted punishment for an injustice." Aneksi and the Pharaoh turned to Kairunamete as he reached out to touch the charm on Aneksi's wrist and turned it over. The symbol that had been etched into it was a bird head. "Often called upon as a servant of Horus, an assassin wielding a falcon-headed saber is sent to haunt and kill his enemies."

"Petbe is only worshipped by those in Akhmin," the Pharaoh said slowly, "in the central region of the Blacklands."

I am only a deliverer, and I bring the news of your death.

Aneksi's heart lurched at the thought of Lithra seeking to destroy her with such means.

Kairunamete nodded.

"And many of those in Akhmin are loyal to the High Priest of Horus." He leveled his gaze with the Pharaoh. "Two consorts who happen to be daughters of the High Priest of Horus -there is our source of power- and also happen to be vying for everything Aneksi has seems to match up quite neatly with the slave's words."

The Pharaoh clenched his jaw, his fingers curling into a fist. "They expect to dishonor their Pharaoh and expect to gain from it," he shook his head in distress.

Kairunamete now turned to Aneksi. "Since we now know your miscarriage was a product of poison, I'll seek out the High Priest of Sekhmet to now provide something to remove any traces of it from you." he stood up, motioning for her to follow.

The Pharaoh stood up with them. The Lord-Priest nodded in his direction.

"I will assume all is well after I leave the Palace," Kairunamete added.

"Of course," the Pharaoh replied. "This will all be over

within the next full moon."

Aneksi was given a detoxifying diet to follow for the next month by Meryt, as Ekmati had been away on an emergency.

While she was there, the Pharaoh called for a meeting with his viziers in the Throne Room. He informed them of Lithra and the two consort's crimes, before requesting that servants fetch Kenbets for their coming trial and have scribes to prepare for it.

Sometime after the servants had left, a Palace guard ran in. He knelt before the men and waited for the Pharaoh to call upon him.

"What is it?" the Pharaoh asked, sitting back in annoyance that he was interrupted.

"Their highnesses, Princess Nebta and Princess Hemetre have, fallen ill, may the gods punish me for bringing such news to you," he answered without looking up.

The Pharaoh straightened and looked in the guard's direction.

"What?" The guard hesitated to speak. "Answer me," the Pharaoh ordered.

"T-the princesses, daughters of Lady Ahset and Lady Akhara-"

"I know who their mothers are," the Pharaoh interrupted with an annoyed growl. "Tell me what happened to them." The guard looked up briefly, tears in his eyes seeing the Pharaoh's open frustration at him.

"Forgive me, I don't know what has afflicted them. I was told only to tell Your Majesty immediately."

The Pharaoh sighed, shaking his head.

"You may go. I'll be there." The guard nodded and did as told. The Pharaoh's viziers turned to face him as he spoke to them. "Don't delay in this trial," the Pharaoh said as he stood up. "I want the Kenbets here before nightfall and a verdict before I rest tonight."

The viziers nodded and bowed their heads as the Pharaoh strode off to see what had befallen on his eldest daughters. He asked his personal guards where the two girls stayed and to lead him there, as he himself did not know.

Ekmati was in the two's adjoined consort chamber, his assistant with him as they rinsed and replaced cooling cloths on the girls' foreheads.

They bowed as the Pharaoh entered.

Upon seeing Ahset and Akhara weeping at the base of their child's bed, he cleared his throat and looked away. He knew they were surely guilty in conspiring against Neferkempi and could not bring himself to look at them. And being as tall as he was, the Pharaoh did not venture far into the chamber; the hanging decorations had hit into him on his way in.

The Pharaoh remained by the doorway. "Can you tell me what has happened, Ekmati?"

"It seems to be a fever, Your Majesty." Ekmati tilted his head. "The cause is unknown."

"Can it be treated still?" the Pharaoh asked.

"I'll do all I can," Ekmati answered, his face devoid of expression. "But I cannot prescribe strong herbs to overpower their fever as they are too young." He paused. "I cannot guarantee survival."

The Pharaoh felt a sliver of fear run down his spine hearing those words.

PART XXIX.

"Your Majesty, how can we agree to have the mothers of your ill children put to trial?" one of the Kenbets asked. The others nodded in agreement. The Kenbets had arrived by sundown and were told of the situation. They sat with the Pharaoh's viziers as well.

The Pharaoh furrowed his eyebrows.

"I will not allow for such treasonous acts to go

unpunished," he shot back, "no matter who it is. I lost my Prince and nearly the Great Royal Wife." The men bowed their heads immediately at the tone of his voice.

"Of course, Your Majesty," they said in unison.

"All the proof we need is here." The Pharaoh gazed at them with slightly narrowed eyes as he continued. "The slave confessed and has been in hiding ever since. Her allegations of poison and being an accomplice match exactly to what caused the termination of the Great Royal Wife's first pregnancy, her kidnapping, and the slave's own change in behavior. These crimes are unpardonable and require the highest degree of punishment." The Pharaoh stopped to allow the men to think. "What is your judgment? I will hear you out."

The men whispered amongst themselves. After a moment or two, the one who spoke first cleared his throat.

"We agree that the evidence is clear. However, if Lady Ahset and Lady Akhara are guilty, we feel execution may be too harsh."

"Too harsh," the Pharaoh echoed.

"Yes, Your Majesty," a Kenbet replied. "With the princesses' health in critical condition and their mothers to be executed, the High Priest of Horus and his followers may see this as an act of hostility."

The Pharaoh pursed his lips at their words.

"Are you suggesting I ignore the rules handed down to me by the gods for the sake of appeasing the High Priest?"

"Of course not, Your Majesty," the men said, bowing their heads.

"Then what are you suggesting?"

"The goddess Meretseger protects the Royal Tombs," one of the other Kenbets said. The Pharaoh raised an eyebrow at his seemingly switch in topics. "She destroys those who think to steal from the Pharaohs of afore. But She also forgives. We find that mercy must be shown upon them, Your Majesty, in the light of their situation."

The Pharaoh let out an exasperated breath. "So, you believe they will show remorse of their crimes because of what has befallen their daughters?"

"In their grievance, yes," the Kenbet said. The others nodded in agreement. "They are on the brink of losing Your children. That alone may sway them to repent and be ashamed."

The Pharaoh sat back, feeling slightly defeated. What they were asking for made perfect sense. But how could he agree? Neferkempi would remain in danger if any of the three were to live.

"What punishment, then, do you agree fits their crimes?" he asked.

A vizier spoke now. "Our say is that the slave be executed, but the High Priest's daughters should be exiled to their Temple, with no affiliation to the Palace or Royal Family."

The Pharaoh tilted his head, finding himself in favor of this. He would be stripping them of the power they had used to manipulate Lithra, taking them away from his children whom they could use for future abuse, and removing their claims to the throne that they had desperately wanted. And their means to accomplish everything so far -Lithra- would now be out of service.

He nodded. "Prepare the Royal Scribes for this trial tomorrow morning."

The night air was cool as Pharaoh walked to his private chamber. He was excited to let Neferkempi know everything would be taken care of and the two could now focus on preparing for the birth of their first child.

The Pharaoh smiled at the thought. Neferkempi would be a wonderful mother. She had endearing patience, was quick to give love, and already showed promise with Ankhetep's affection for her. Being a mother to his children would also help Neferkempi learn the ways of the court.

As he continued down the hall, something flew past the Pharaoh's front guard, smashing against the candles that lit the hall. It was quickly followed by several more, and a grey haze clouded the air, obscuring their vision, before the candle fires blew out. In the darkness, the Pharaoh froze, hearing metal clank against the wall with force and something brush past his side.

Four Palace guards rushed over with torches and spears in hand. The Pharaoh glanced about, seeing his personal guards knocked out against the wall, each sporting an open head wound.

"What's going on?" the Pharaoh demanded, breathing hard. Was this an attack on the Palace? "Is Neferkempi safe? Go and find out!" Two guards ran to do as ordered while the rest relit the candles and examining the thrown objects.

The Pharaoh took a step forward when he felt something beneath his sandal. Bending over, he retrieved a piece of paper. With narrowed eyes he read:

You will never find me. But I am desperate to tell you what I have done through my own lips, Your Greatness. I will give myself up, only if you grant me this chance. I will be at the Royal Tombs in the darkest hour of the night. No guards.

Just you and me.

The Pharaoh looked up at the sound of a dozen more Palace guards arriving to surround him. The Chief Guard knelt before him; head bowed.

"Your Majesty, we were unable to find the harasser. We deserve death for endangering your life," the Chief Guard lamented.

"Is Nefekempi safe?" the Pharaoh asked, crumpling the note into his fist.

"Your Majesty," the Chief Guard said, his head remained bowed.

"Take me to her. Now."

Aneski sat upright at the swarm of guards that entered the private chamber. She held the sheets up against her breast, her heart racing.

"What is the meaning of this?" she asked, eyebrows furrowed.

"Neferkempi!" Aneksi turned to see the guards part away to allow the Pharaoh through. He rushed to her side, grasping her free hand. "Are you alright?" he asked, his frantic eyes searching her face.

"Yes, of course." Aneksi gave him a quick smile and

squeezed his hand. "Why? Has something happened?"

"Neferkempi," the Pharaoh sighed, pulling her into a sudden embrace. He pulled away and she glanced down, her cheeks flushed, as all the guards were still in the chamber. "Stay on alert," the Pharaoh ordered the guards.

In response, they clanked the end of their spears against the ground in unison and filed out of the chamber.

The Pharaoh settled himself under the sheets, laying his head on her chest. Aneksi wrapped her arms around him, as he pressed against her with eyes shut.

"Tell me, what's the matter?" she asked after several silent moments, concerned about the Pharaoh's behavior.

He opened his eyes and looked up at Aneksi.

"I don't know what to do," he whispered. He lifted his hand and showed her the wrinkled scrap of paper in his fist. "In all my life, I have never been so unsure of this world."

Aneksi took it from him and flattened it out to read. Her eyes widened immediately, recognizing the handwriting.

"It's from Lithra," the Pharaoh said. Aneksi swallowed hard and looked down at his dark eyes. "She attacked my guards to give me this message. I feared she came for you." Aneksi tossed the paper aside to hold the Pharaoh tighter, pressing him against her body. Tears pricked her eyes.

217

"I am safe," she whispered, feeling her throat constrict. "Your baby is safe."

"Oh, Neferkempi, what do I do?"

PART XXX.

Aneksi let a servant put a shawl over her bare shoulders as another went to fetch Meryt. She stared out at the entrance to the private garden, where the Pharaoh had previously exited.

If Lithra loved him as she said she did, she would not harm the Pharaoh. Aneksi placed one hand over her growing abdomen and the second curled into a fist. She would have this child, and by doing so, would prove to all those within the Palace who harbored Lithra's sentiment that they could not bring her down.

"Lady Meryt is here," she heard Rai call out from behind the door. Meryt entered a moment later, bowing her head. Aneksi stood up from the bed and forced a smile, indicating that they sit down.

"Thank you for coming so quickly at this time."

Meryt nodded. "Of course. I was already up making sure the princesses were sent home from the medicinal chambers."

"Already?" Aneksi raised an eyebrow. "I was told they were severely ill earlier today."

"Grandfather believes the worst of their fever has passed. They should wake up healthy from a night of rest."

Aneksi frowned slightly. "I approved for a ceremony of well-wishes for the sake of the princesses' health tomorrow."

"Their quick recovery was unexpected for me," Meryt curled a lock of hair behind her ear. "I've never seen anything like it. But isn't it too late to cancel the event? Now that they are in good health?" she asked. Aneksi nodded. "The offerings are supposed to be sent to the High Priest of Horus at the end of the ceremony, yes?" Aneksi nodded again. Meryt shook her head. "Alright, then, so how can I help you? I brought you some herbs if the child was bringing you discomfort."

Aneksi shook her head. "It's not that. I asked you here because so much has happened...and I'd like someone to stay at my side right now."

Meryt nodded and took a seat. "Then I shall stay here as long as you'd like me to."

The Pharaoh stood outside the Royal Tomb, feeling the cold night winds stronger tonight. His arms were crossed over his chest and feet stood apart. The stars dotted the sky above him; but there was no moonlight to illuminate the earth.

Torches staked across the outer entrance blazed by the tomb, the winds scattering loose sands in volleys.

She walked out of the dark horizon with poise, her blue eyes glittering. She was dressed in a plain cream linen dress that reached to her shins and a belt buckle about her waist.

The Pharaoh narrowed his eyes in contempt. After all she had done, how could she still hold her head high in his presence?

Lithra stopped to stand a few yards away from the Pharaoh. She bowed her head, her long brown hair rising and settling with the changing winds. When she looked up, she smiled.

"I thank you for coming to see me," Lithra whispered. The Pharaoh's brow wrinkled, wondering if the distance had made him mishear her words. Him see her? It was far from it. Tears now formed in Lithra's eyes. "I knew you loved me. From the bottom of your heart, you truly, truly do."

The Pharaoh jerked back, twisting his body in outright disgust. "What did you say?"

"Why else would you come," Lithra went on, ignoring his question, "if you didn't?" The Pharaoh shook his head, unable to find words. Seeing this, Lithra continued, moved by the Pharaoh's willingness to respond to her. "I knew you'd come. I knew it because it tears your heart knowing of the things I have done, and you do not want to believe it."

"Lithra-!"

"Of course, you think me innocent." Lithra's tears were streaming down her face now, but it was hard for the Pharaoh to make out with the fires behind him shifting to and fro, giving him only glimpses of her face. "And I'm here to say we can run away together. Live-"

"Silence!" the Pharaoh roared, startling Lithra. "How dare you speak to me so freely after taking Ahmose from me? This ends here, o wretched slave. I don't know what's cursed your mind, but whatever it is, it is no concern of mine. I've only come to destroy you. I ask that Ammut devour your black heart for all eternity."

"What-?"

The Pharaoh raised an arm. His personal guards released the arrows that had been taut against their string. In the darkness, they sailed through the cold night air with a hiss.

Lithra took a stumbled step back at the onslaught. She swayed in place, staring down at the six arrows embedded inside her torso and stomach, her dress quickly darkening.

The Pharaoh watched her fall to her knees.

"You betrayed me," she mouthed silently.

The guards lowered their bows just as she withdrew something from her belt. Before anyone could react, Lithra hurled the obsidian blade directly at the Pharaoh before she fell to the ground. The Pharaoh's eyes widened as the blade came in contact with his left shoulder, too stunned to do anything else.

The Pharaoh's guards shouted and rushed as he dropped to the ground, while others hurried to bring a chariot to take him back to safety. One of his guards lifted the Pharaoh upright in his arms, desperate to keep him conscious.

Anit, the Pharaoh's longest-serving personal guard, dropped his bow to the sandy ground and walked over to Lithra's hunched body. He glared hard at Lithra, fuming at the treachery he had just witnessed. The recently stitched wound on his head no longer pained him. He grabbed her by her hair and with his free hand, unclipped the short sword at his belt. With a firm motion, he dug it into her throat and wrenched it across her neck.

The Pharaoh brought a shaking hand to the wound, feeling a warmth trickle down his fingers. He felt his heart stammer and vision blur.

Neferkempi. Would she lose him, too?

He collapsed into his guard's arms.

PART XXXI.

The Pharaoh went in and out of consciousness all night. Ekmati and Nekure removed the blade and cleaned the wound; while there was no poison present, the Pharaoh's loss of blood was untreatable. Lithra's dagger had hit the flesh that connected the whole of his arm to his chest.

The Pharaoh's viziers came together for a meeting immediately after the Pharaoh's entry back into the Palace. Standing at his side in the surgical hall, they debated over what to do until his recovery.

"I say we keep this news to ourselves and find some way to have all matters handled by us," one of them suggested. "The Crown Prince is barely five years of age; he cannot take after his father."

"But it's our duty to grant the Heir Prince his right to the throne in times like this," a second vizier countered.

"I disagree. If we allow the Heir Prince to assume leadership, the Great Royal Wife will serve as his Regent. And she knows nothing about running this nation!" a third called out, pinching the bridge of his nose.

"Perhaps the Heir Prince's mother should be instated?" the fourth wondered aloud. The men fell silent for a moment.

"His Majesty would not like it if Lady Kiya surpassed the

Great Royal Wife," the second finally said.

"But what truly is his chance of survival?" the third said in a low voice. "I say we have the Heir Prince become Pharaoh Tempore with his mother as Regent. If the Great Royal Wife bears a son before His Majesty recovers, we shall demote Lady Kiya. If he doesn't recover-"

"Her Highness's father will come for us," the first vizier said shaking his head, "once news breaks out that we have chosen a consort over the Great Royal Wife."

The third vizier pinched the bridge of his nose at such a concern. The other three waited for his reply.

"You know as well as I that the Lord-Priest cannot refute anything we have discussed," he said. "The Great Royal Wife's inexperience in political affairs makes her a despicable choice for leadership. It would be simpler for the Temple of Isis to assume the power as they have for the past fifty years."

"How do we tell this to Her Highness without bringing harm to her?" the fourth vizier asked. "Her fragility is a matter of concern."

"Exactly why Lady Kiya should be Regent," the third vizier said, hitting his fist against his palm. "We will tell the Lord-Priest that Her Highness needs to be at rest in such dramatic times and Lady Kiya will only serve Regent until Her

Highness has her child."

"I don't believe telling Her Highness the truth of His Majesty's condition is a wise decision," the first vizier said. "His survival is uncertain."

"Actually, it may as well fall in our favor." The third vizier smiled. "Allow me to deal with it."

Aneksi woke up with a chill. It was her first night without sleeping with her father's charm and she had no nightmare, yet something would not settle in her chest. Her head was throbbing, and she did not have the drive to get up or call a servant.

She slowly turned to face the dark ceiling, an arm splayed out in the direction of where the Pharaoh should have been. Aneksi sighed aloud and closed her eyes again. Of course, the Pharaoh was alright. Why wouldn't he be?

Aneksi remained as she was for a time, drifting into a light slumber until a thunderous noise broke her peace.

Ankhetep marched into the chamber from the private garden with baby Ka-Rae in his arms. A concerned Epishert followed after him with her hands clasped tightly in front of her. As Aneksi rose from the bed to receive them, she froze at the sight of another woman angrily following after the two boys.

Kiya.

She was adorned in her usual array of jewels and wearing a tight-fitted cotton gown to match. Kiya still wore her white and blue headdress Temple if Isis headdress, perhaps in a reminder that she was a mother to a prince twice over.

Kiya stood by the entranceway with her arms crossed over her half-exposed breast. Her eyes flittered around the room with a deep frown. Aneksi knew she was expecting the Pharaoh to have been here. Ankhetep skipped inside the chamber, unaware of his mother's disapproval.

"Your Highness, my prince brother cries too often," Ankhetep said as he held out Ka-Rae. Aneksi hesitated knowing Kiya was in the chamber but took the child into her arms anyway. As she did so, Ankhetep quickly climbed onto the bed now that his arms were free.

"They all do, Ankhetep." Aneksi's voice was low and her body was still rigid knowing that Kiya would be listening in on what they spoke of.

"For what purpose?" he asked, watching Aneksi slowly rock the child. Aneksi stared at the sleeping baby's face, feeling calmed by it. She faced Ankhetep again.

"That's how they speak. If Ka-Rae didn't scream so often,

how would the servants know he is hungry? When he is in discomfort in his bed?"

"Speaking of beds, my prince brother stole mine." At this, Ankhetep crossed his arms over his chest and turned his head away.

Aneksi smiled. "Did he?"

"Yes. Father ordered he sleep where I once did. I now rest in an unbecoming chamber."

"Ankhetep, you are growing up so quickly. Ka-Rae is only following after you as his guide. You should accept this change wholeheartedly."

Ankhetep looked at Aneksi and then turned his head back.

"Well, as Heir Prince, I don't appreciate this justified behavior," he firmly replied. "I'm more than disappointed that you are in favor of it." Aneksi laughed. How was it possible for one to be so young yet also so serious? Her childhood was nothing like this. Ankhetep glanced her way, both pleased and shocked at the sound. "Actually, my disappointment is now gone. Your laugh is as wonderful as you are."

Kiya made a strangled scoff in her throat. Aneksi blinked, remembering she was still here and blushed furiously in embarrassment.

"Father always said to be truthful as one can be," Ankhetep noted, eyebrows furrowed at the reactions he received for his comment. Aneksi shook her head but could not hold back a genuine smile.

"But you mustn't give praise so quickly," she advised. "There must only be a numbered few who should attain your devotion."

Ankhetep nodded. "And you are among them."

"That's enough for today," Kiya's voice cut between the two. Aneksi pursed her lips and looked down at Ka-Rae. "Her Highness must be made to look presentable now. Off we go, my Heir Prince."

Ankhetep made a low, guttural noise of contempt and mumbled a "Her Highness looks presentable already" but did as he was told. He slid off the bed and slipped on his sandals to walk over to Kiya's side. Epehshert quietly walked up to Aneksi and took Ka-Rae back. Aneksi swallowed hard, for some reason feeling grief-stricken now that her arms were empty.

"I didn't ask about Her Highness' baby yet," Ankhetep said. Kiya took hold of his hand and began walking out.

"Save that for another day, my Heir Prince."

The two exited, closely followed by Epehshert.

Aneksi sighed. She had forgotten how uplifting Ankhetep was to her. As she stepped out of bed, her servants came forward to dress her for the day.

The Pharaoh wasn't present during breakfast. Aneksi felt the other wives narrow their eyes at her, suspecting she knew his whereabouts while they did not. Aneksi kept a straight face and focused her gaze on her food as she herself did not know why he had not come back yet.

Aneksi called the viziers to a meeting in the Throne room after breakfast. They stood before her, calm and hands folded in front of them.

"You were all the last to see the Pharaoh after his return last night, is this true?" Aneksi asked. The men bowed their heads in acknowledgment. Aneksi narrowed her eyes and her voice grew stern. "Then tell me where he is."

One of the four viziers spoke up.

"I would first ask that you think of the health of the child you carry," he began. Aneksi tilted her head, bringing her hand to her abdomen. "We, unfortunately, lost one to the gods already-"

Aneksi slammed her fist against the armrest in a burst of anger. Something must have happened if they were not answering her outright.

"Where is he? What happened last night?"

The vizier hesitated only the slightest bit.

"His Majesty is dying, Your Highness." Aneksi gasped at his words. "We feared for your health and so delayed your notice. Forgive us, we deserve to be punished." Aneksi shook her head, eyes watering.

"No...how? How?" Aneksi swallowed hard, blinking away tears. Did Lithra hurt him? Of course, she did. There was no other explanation. But why? Aneksi looked back at the viziers. "I cannot see him?"

"Unfortunately, no, Your Highness...unless you sign this Temporary Leave of Absence."

The vizier turned away to retrieve the Royal Scribe's tablet and present it to Aneksi.

"Signing here, Heir Prince Ankhetep will be instated as Pharaoh Tempore and someone we have voted will serve as his Regent while you are away at His Majesty's side."

Aneksi reached out for the quill being offered to her. "And this is the only way I can see him?"

The same vizier answered.

"Yes, otherwise we will begin preparations for your Regency Ceremony immediately. There will be no time to see

His Majesty among the many threats that may arise from this transfer of titles."

"And we must set to finish His Majesty's building construction immediately after that," chimed in another vizier.

"And appoint new priests–" another began.

"Do not forget the well-wishes Ceremony!" interrupted another.

"What about the–"

"Alright," Aneksi cut them off with an exasperated sigh. She glanced at Rai, who had been frowning during the entire time. "I understand what's being asked of me." Aneksi paused to stare at the document held out before her. The viziers knew what they were doing. Surely their pick for Regent would be a much better suit than she was.

Aneksi briefly closed her eyes. Her father would not be happy with her signing off a Leave of Absence. But she had to. Aneksi could not imagine herself ruling without the Pharaoh or find any solace at night knowing she was away from him when he needed her the most.

The moment the tip of the quill had lifted from the papyrus, it was stamped with the Seal of the Great Royal Wife and quickly taken away. The viziers bowed as Aneksi stood up.

"I'd like to see the Pharaoh now," she said. The men nodded and indicated for her to exit.

Aneksi exhaled lightly and forced a smile. Away from prying, devious eyes, she knew she would be far safer at the Pharaoh's side than being surrounded by people she did not know and would have her baby's life away from the forefront of any rising enemy to the throne.

PART XXXII.

She was taken to an underground chamber below the medicinal chambers. Several sconces were lit along the mossy stone walls, dousing the bedchamber in a bright yellow-orange hue.

"Neferkempi? What are you doing here?"

The Pharaoh saw Neferkempi freeze for a second at the doorway, her hands bunched together at her sides to lift the ends of her dress. She then raced over to him, kneeling by the bedside.

"Oh, thank the gods, you're alright!" she cried. The Pharaoh's face broke into a smile and he gently leaned forward to touch his forehead to hers.

"Yes, of course, I am," he said, drawing away to gaze into

her eyes. He moved his good arm to run his finger along her jawline. "Would I leave you without having even seen our first child born?"

Neferkempi shook her head, her tears spilling through.

"They told me you were dying; how could I not worry?" she whispered. "I feared for so many things-"

She was cut off by the Pharaoh flicking her nose with his thumb.

"I'm not too ill, I do not want to see you fretting over it," he said, hoping she would not suspect him to lie. "I will be alright." Neferkempi let out a sigh and wrinkled her nose as she looked away.

The Pharaoh's lips tugged into a smile seeing her frustrated. She was relieved to be told he was in no serious condition but also upset her worries were brushed aside.

"Come here," he said, indicating with his uninjured hand to the bed beside him. She did as told and leaned into him as the Pharaoh pressed his lips to the side of her head, flinching. "I will be alright," he repeated.

But the pain in his left shoulder had returned. He could even feel fresh blood trickling down his arm.

"Swear by the gods you will be," Neferkempi whispered, looking into his eyes. The Pharaoh dropped his gaze to their joined hands.

"Neferkempi, I wish that you only worry for yourself and the future of our child. To worry over me will be too burdensome." The Pharaoh sighed at her silence. "I expect my viziers have spoken to you about instating Ankhetep?" She nodded this time. "You must be strong and have faith. As his Regent, most -if not all- decisions will fall upon you. This is something I know you can learn to do." When she did not reply, the Pharaoh furrowed his eyebrows. "What is it? Why aren't you replying to this?"

He felt Neferkempi curl away from him.

"I declined," she said in a low voice. The Pharaoh tilted his head, confused.

"What?"

She closed her eyes briefly. "The viziers had me sign a Leave of Absence. It was the only way I could see you-"

"Neferkempi!" the Pharaoh stared at her, wide-eyed. She jumped at the loudness in his voice and turned her gaze towards the Pharaoh. The pain in his shoulder seemed to intensify with every passing moment. "A Leave of Absence means you have been exiled from the Palace until a request is made for your return. If someone sees you still here, you will be found guilty of breaking a Royal decree!" The Pharaoh shook his head, blinking rapidly. "I don't understand, I know you're unaware of this but why would they..." he trailed off. He would never have suspected his viziers to be so deceitful.

Aneksi felt her blood run cold at the Pharaoh's words.

"They lied-?" she whispered. The Pharaoh looked at her.

"Yes, and you must find someone to tell Ankhetep to write for your reentry at once," he said in a rush.

"Well, it's alright," she assured him, "I don't mind staying away from the Palace while the child within me grows. I feel that would be safer-"

"No." The Pharaoh shook his head, looking paler by the second. Aneksi took his hand and took it into her lap. He was shivering. Why was he so worried?

"I'll stay with my father until you recover. This isn't so much of a troublesome thing," she assured him.

"Oh, Neferkempi," the Pharaoh said, his eyes softening. She smiled at him, squeezing his hand. He leaned over and gently pressed his lips to hers. Aneksi closed her eyes, momentarily forgetting the peril she had just walked into.

PART XXXIII.

When Aneksi had climbed back up the dark stairwell, the viziers and a dozen Palace guards greeted her. Upon reaching them, she held her head high. These were the men who had knowingly tricked her.

Two of the viziers did not meet her gaze. The other two met hers with a look of feigned ignorance.

"Your Highness will follow these guards and be safely escorted to the Lord-Priest's residence," one said. "All of your belongings have been situated for travel."

Aneksi squared her shoulders. "I will not leave until I have an audience with the Heir Prince."

The viziers shared a look.

"Of course, Your Highness," one of the other viziers replied.

"But time is of the essence," cut in the vizier who spoke first. "His Young Majesty will have but little leisure to speak so freely with Your Highness."

Aneksi narrowed her eyes at him but followed them anyway. The Pharaoh had instructed her what to tell Ankhetep just in case his recovery took longer than expected.

The Heir Prince was being fitted for his imperial robes when Aneksi was given five minutes to speak with him.

"Your Highness!" Ankhetep cried, his face darkening in a blush. Aneksi smiled at his boyish embarrassment and bowed her head, gazing away from him, where he stood with his upper body exposed. "You may leave," he instructed the servants.

When they had gone, Aneksi sighed at the amount of trust and responsibility she would have to endow to the young Pharaoh Tempore. But before she could speak, Ankhetep asked, "How is my father? The viziers refuse my request to see him."

Aneksi looked over at the boy, feeling her heart sink at his voice.

"Your father is doing as well as he can. But right now, he's expecting good to come of your current reign." Ankhetep's lips quivered. Aneksi opened her mouth to reassure him, but he had already begun to sob. "Oh, no, no," She murmured before she knelt by the young Pharaoh-to-be. She placed one light hand on his shoulder and the other to move his hand away from his face to wipe away his tears. "Why do cry, Ankhetep?"

He sniffed, keeping his eyes locked on the floor.

"I'm afraid I will disappoint my father," he whispered. "Sometimes... Sometimes I wish I were a servant boy, just so my father would also be one and not expect so much from me." Aneksi smiled at him.

"Your father loves you, Ankhetep. And for that reason,

no matter what you do, he will always see greatness in you."

Ankhetep looked up at her and sniffed. "Truly?"

Aneksi nodded.

"Yes, by Ma'at."

Ankhetep exhaled loudly then stood up straighter. "Then I will rule the Blacklands like my father: with an iron fist and an open heart."

"Why rule with an iron fist?" Aneksi asked, seeing that his tears had stopped flowing and his voice was slowly regaining its composure.

"Because the authority of the Pharaoh and His Palace must never be questioned."

"And why with an open heart?"

"Because father said only with an open heart he was able to meet a woman who appeared to be a servant, fell in love with her and then named her his Great Royal Wife."

Aneksi felt her chest prick with a bittersweet feeling at his words.

"I want to be exactly like my father so when he returns, he will tell me: 'I am proud of you, Ankhetep.'"

The chamber door screeched open, followed by the marching in of the Palace guards and the rushing sweep of the viziers' robes. Aneksi's eyes widened, realizing she had forgotten to speak to Ankhetep about her leaving.

Ankhetep made a reach for her when he saw her being grabbed by the Palace guards.

"Your Highness!"

"Ankhetep, you must visit me when you learn of your sibling's birth," Aneksi called out to him.

"Let her go! What are you doing?" Ankhetep ignored her, shouting at the men.

"Ankhetep! Look at me!" She was halfway to the door, dragging her feet to slow her exit down. Ankhetep finally caught her gaze. "I will be fine! But I beg you, seek me out by the next harvest, please seek me out!"

But by then, Aneksi had been shoved out the door. How much he had heard above the clank of the guards' spears and armor, she could only hope.

Aneksi was then carried off into a palanquin. There was no ceremony or official farewell and she was jostled out of the Palace before she could even notify Meryt of what was going on. It took all of Aneksi's energy not to break down and weep in the darkness of the shielded palanquin. Instead, she cradled herself and closed her eyes, praying for the best.

Kairunamete rushed down from the Tri-God Temple steps to approach the unplanned visitors. His shoulders were straightened, and chest puffed, the smell of fermented beer and cultivated wine strong in the air.

"What is the meaning of this!" he shouted. Aneksi pursed her lips at her father's open display of raw emotion. It was unlike him. The vizier that had joined Aneksi en route to her exile folded his hands behind his back and bowed.

"Her Highness signed a Leave of Absence in the wake of His Majesty's illness." Aneksi perked up at the words, feeling her father's sharp gaze her way. "She'll remain with Your Lordship as it was signed in the contract."

"Where is this decree?" Kairunamete growled. "My daughter should be leading this nation with the Pharaoh away!"

"I'll request for a copy to be sent to you, Your Lordship." The vizier nodded and began to turn away. "Farewell."

Aneksi watched in horror as her father grabbed the vizier by his tunic, brandishing some weapon. Around them, the Palace guards tensed but hesitated on who was the more powerful of the two.

"I won't be mocked by the likes of you Isis worshippers," Kairunamete hissed. He shoved the vizier away, forcing the man to stumble before he caught his footing. "When I have settled all of this, you shall be the first to die. Give me my daughter and leave my sight."

Aneksi felt her heart hammer painfully in her chest as the Palace guards drew her out of the palanquin. She had never once feared her father; she had no need to. Aneksi remained standing before the Lord-Priest, head bowed and timid as the vizier adjusted his tunic and left without another word.

Once gone, Kairunamete grabbed Aneksi by her hair and wrenched her forward, heading towards the temple. Aneksi let out a scream as pain shot up her scalp and she squirmed under his grasp, trying to claw away his hand.

"Please, Father, let me go!" Aneksi cried. "Please-!"

Kairunamete pushed her away, cutting her off. Aneksi fell ungracefully to the ground, breathing hard. She curled an arm around her belly and whimpered.

"I did everything for you," the Lord-Priest seethed. "Everything. Your entire being is because of me. And yet your naïveté has cost us all that I have worked to achieve. You have disgraced me. This Temple. The gods we serve to uphold."

"I'm sorry," Aneksi whispered through her tears. "I'm so sorry-"

"You truly are dull-witted. The slave of yours had more cunning than you." Aneksi clenched her jaw at the mention of Lithra, shutting her eyes. "Get up, Aneksi. Your child still holds potential."

Three servants ran to Aneksi's aid after her father had stepped away.

"The Master had a celebratory drink when news reached that the Heir Prince Ankhetep would need a regent for his reign," one said. "He means no harm."

Aneksi swallowed. Of course not. Her father would never rationally think so ill of her or want to harm her.

The other two were silent as they brought her to her feet. Aneksi wiped away her tears with the back of her hand, staring hard in the direction of her father.

The coming months would be trying indeed.

PART XXXIV.

Four months later

"Remember, this child belongs to the Pharaoh!" the visiting priestess from the Temple of Hathor said for the tenth time. But with every heave, Aneksi felt her strength slip away. The saffron powder and beer mixture swathed upon her belly did not seem to help the delivery as her father had said it would. Beneath her was a painted birthing brick; the same one her mother had used to bring her into the world.

Aneksi was in the newly refurnished birth-arbor beside

the Tri-God Temple. It was too dark to see properly, as the thick matted roof built was to shade her from the harsh light of Ra. The birth-arbor smelled of the imported wood from the pillars raised high to support it. Curling vines were engraved around their top, but Aneksi had barely noticed them. Along the walls were colored drawings of various gods and goddesses, among them being Hathor, drawn as a cow; Bes, a dwarf; Taweret, a hippopotamus; and Meskhenet, in the form of a birthing brick with a human head.

Each of the Pharaoh's wives had gotten through this. And Kiya twice.

Aneksi gripped the floor and blinked away the sticky and salty moisture out of her eyes. She could not tell if it were sweat from the strenuous pushing or tears from the unending pain raking up her body. Her hair was stringy and wet, some strands plastered to her forehead and others hanging about her face. The air was suffocating her and had been for some time.

Four other women were with Aneksi in the single chamber. One had been sent from the Temple of Hathor to aid Aneksi in her labor and the other three were servants from a nearby temple dedicated to Tawaret, the goddess of pregnant women and childbirth. Two sat by each of her sides, holding her shoulders, giving small praises and shoulder and arm rubs. Another sat in front of her to catch the child and the last waved the clouds from steaming water in Aneksi's direction.

None seemed to be truly helping. Aneksi had fooled herself when the pains of labor first began, thinking it was not so bad. But several hours later, the pain had increased and remained that way. The entire night had gone by and still no baby. Aneksi tried to sit back and shut her eyes -tell the women she could not go through with this- but with each attempt at quitting came with a sharp stab of pain that forced her back into reality.

"...Make the heart of the deliverer strong and keep alive the one that is coming."

Aneksi was too preoccupied to hear everything the woman from the Temple of Hathor said. It was a spell of some sort.

"I see it, Your Highness! Steady! It's almost over!"

Aneksi let out a sigh, which sounded more like a disgruntled yell. Through a set of fresh tears, she whispered the Pharaoh's name. He was counting on her to do this without him at her side.

Aneksi was unsure of what happened next, but the cry of

a newborn sent the four women into a frenzy. She at first could not understand the excitement, as she was too stunned from the sudden momentary relief that flooded her body.

The maidservants quickly cut the umbilical cord and began cleaning up both mother and child. While one of the women washed the screeching baby, Aneksi and the other women waited out for the afterbirth. At last, the child was placed into Aneksi's arms.

The women dropped their gazes in somber disappointment.

"It's a girl," one of them said.

Aneksi held onto the small bundle, smiling through her exhaustion and tears.

"Azeneth," she whispered, looking up at the women before her and pressing the girl close to her breast. Aneksi let out a small laugh of pure joy at the circumstance. The women glanced at each other, brows knitted in confusion at Aneksi's happiness for a girl and not a boy. She knew the perfect name for her. "Azeneth. She who belongs to her father."

The child was taken away to be nursed and Aneksi went in and out of consciousness for most of the morning as she had lost too much blood. Her thoughts constantly drifted to her past, during the times she was unknowingly courting with the Pharaoh.

"He seems like a good man," Lithra was saying. Aneksi blinked up at her, previously staring into the ground, daydreaming.

"What? Who?"

"The Pharaoh."

"Oh. Well, I'm not fond of the idea that he's been returning so frequently these days. You're supposed to drive him away, remember?" Aneksi said.

Lithra looked away. "He's good company."

"Oh, Lithra-"

"Can't I even enjoy that?" Lithra snapped.

"Well, of course." Aneksi shrugged. Lithra sighed.

"So how is your mysterious courtier? Has he told you his name today?"

Aneksi smiled at the mention of him. She turned her head up to look at the white canopy that shrouded the Temple, churning above them in the wind.

"When someone has a place in your heart, do they really need a name?"

Lithra raised an eyebrow at Aneksi's answer and then laughed. "I'll take that as a no."

PART XXXV.

The Lord-Priest held his head in his hands, distraught. A girl?

How could the gods punish him with this? A naive daughter and now a granddaughter who secured only doubt to the throne. He raised his head up at the three statues he had been kneeling to for the duration of Aneksi's labor. The braziers around him had burned nonstop -at least, to him, it seemed so- and now the rays of Ra would outshine them. His knees were weak, and he could barely feel them.

Everything was happening too quickly. The Pharaoh's sudden and continued ill health had drastically changed his plans. Aneksi was still in exile for the last four months with only a single letter from the Palace. And he was too busy trying to quell uprisings among his farmers who resided by the Nile to look into it all.

Kairunamete turned back to face the priestess from the Temple of Hathor who had brought the news to him. She stood with her head bowed and hands folded in front of her. Her youthful face had the marks of a weary and disappointing labor. It was nearing daybreak, and the sky was painted in streaks of pink and white behind her.

"You'll remain here for the time being," Kairunamete said, "so rest now." The maidservant furrowed her eyebrows in confusion, no doubt thinking her duties to help Her Highness would be immediate. But she followed after two of

Kairunamete's servants, who directed her towards the guest chambers. Neither met her questioning gaze.

The Lord-Priest glanced once more at the statues of Ma'at, Ra, and Osiris, and said his farewell so he could visit his daughter. A servant came forward to help him get to his feet and regain composure. With each step Kairunamete took, he fumbled for the right words to express his frustration and disappointment to Aneksi. He wondered if any of the nearby servant women had recently given birth to a boy he could claim as hers. How much would it cost to silence the family forever? A bale of wheat? A sack of gold? Terror?

Upon seeing Aneksi sitting upright in bed with a child in her arms, the storm in his chest came to a staggering calm. Kairunamete blinked several times, unable to fathom the sudden change in his heart. Aneksi was cradling a honey-toned bundle in her arms and lazily gave the little thing forehead and nose kisses. A feeling of wholeness washed over Kairunamete, so much so that he felt it rise in his throat and threatened to erupt out of him as a sob.

Aneksi glanced up from Azeneth's sleeping face hearing her father clear his throat. She smiled a little at the mistiness in his eyes. She looked back down at the baby girl in her arms.

"Your grandfather is here to see you, Azeneth," she

whispered. "Let Mama sleep now. He'll see to you."

Aneksi handed the newborn to her father, who took the child with the utmost gentleness. The other two maidservants helped her to settle into the makeshift bed they had brought into the birth-arbor. Aneksi would stay here for a week under the protection of the gods and goddesses.

By sundown, news of Aneksi's birth rippled from town to town, merchant to merchant.

The peasants who brought in their due harvests doubled their normal amount. The fishermen and huntsmen gave a third more of fish and prey than asked of them. Children brought flowers and dolls and the women brought reed woven baskets, shoes, toys and sewn blankets and tiny dresses for the newborn.

Kairunamete welcomed them and praised their generosity. He promised the gods would favor them and even allowed a few of the men to enter the Tri-God Temple and place their gifts outside the birth-arbor. Aneksi was awake by this time and was grateful to hear that so many showed their support for her. She was especially pleased, knowing that her father's public announcement was open about Azeneth's gender and that had not stopped them from celebrating.

Aneksi had been quite active during her later months of

pregnancy, speaking with farmers, smiths, traders, other priests, guards, and wealthy women. She asked of their likes and dislikes, what their future held for them and what could she do in her power to make it happen. It was no doubt their offerings were a symbol of their trust and admiration for her that she had earned from them. She had also gained much-needed knowledge of governance from her outings.

Aneksi had vowed to herself that she would not allow for what happened in the past to repeat itself when she returned to the Palace. What ate at Aneksi's heart all the while, however, was the Pharaoh's continued lack of communication. A week after her exile, she received a short, unsigned letter from the Palace. It had read:

My Neferkempi,

Stay strong for our child. I have no doubt that he will be wonderful in all accounts. I swear upon the gods that I will love you forever.

No other letters had come addressed to her from the Palace. Aneksi had read it over a dozen times, desperately wishing for there to be more, and trying to decipher it as if it contained some hidden meaning.

Was he alright? Had his wound progressed into

something worse? Was that why he did not mention it?

Some two weeks after giving birth, Aneksi's desperation gave way to hope when her chamber door creaked wide open later one morning.

"Your Highness!" he cried, arms up in the air. "I have come for you!" Aneksi forced herself up, looking at Ankhetep with tired eyes. "Aren't you glad to see me, Your Highness?"

"Of course I am," Aneksi said, patting the bed to invite him.

Aneksi leaned against her arm and watched as the young boy raced up. He was wearing lead paint around his eyes; his thin arms were banded with gold, as was the girdle around his abdomen that hooked his pressed white cotton tunic together. The look of a pharaoh, she smiled, and the heart of one.

"It was quite boring without you," Ankhetep confessed once he settled beside Aneksi. Her smile grew, and she drew a hand to run it across his shaven head down to his cheek.

"Have you been well?"

Ankhetep pinched the bridge of his nose. Aneksi tilted her head at this new gesture.

"No, no, I should've asked that first." He straightened in his place. "How are you and my new sibling? Where is he?"

"She," Aneksi corrected. "You have a younger sister."

"Oh." Ankhetep pressed his lips into a firm line. "Will you allow her to spend time with me?"

"Azeneth is your sister. Of course you may spend time with her," Aneksi said with a smile.

"Hmm." He paused in deep thought, a hand on his chin. He looked back at Aneksi. "You wouldn't mind me teaching her how to throw rocks a far distance?" Aneksi shook her head. "What about picking apart insects?"

"You may teach her anything you wish her to," Aneksi answered with a small laugh.

Ankhetep's face brightened. "This is great! Where is she? Can we begin now?"

"She's a baby, Ankhetep. For now, all she will do is sleep the days away." Ankhetep's shoulders slumped and he pouted, crossing his arms over his chest. Aneksi placed a hand on his cheek. "Now tell me, how is your father?"

Ankhetep looked up at Aneksi with wide eyes. He was now gripping his arms.

"What do you mean, Your Highness? Father was buried two weeks after you left the Palace."

PART XXXVI.

"I did wonder why you did not come to my coronation or to the funeral," Ankhetep continued in a lower tone.

But his words were lost. Aneksi's mind had already wandered into an abysmal corner. Ankhetep never lied; he had no reason to. But how could what he said possibly be true?

"Oh gods," Aneksi clutched her chest, the blood draining from her face. She had lived months unaware that the Pharaoh was gone. She had lived with a smile every morning, thinking about her return. She had lived while he was *dead*.

Ankhetep nudged his face into the crook of her arm and hugged her. "Your Highness," he whispered.

The two mourned in silence together for a time, not in the reassurance that things would be okay, but rather they had no idea how to put into words their loss.

"You'll be coming back with me, right, Your Highness?" Ankhetep asked, looking up at Aneksi. She let her shoulders fall but forced a brief smile the boy's way. He was looking at her intently as if he were taking note of how to act.

Aneksi knew if she grieved too much in front of the boy, it would only keep him from his duties. He would think it was alright to weep and be sad whenever it entered his heart. But

Aneksi's lips trembled. Hiding grief could bring about an early death, knowing her own mother had done the same, and Aneksi could not let the same happen to Ankhetep.

"Ankhetep, I want you to go back to the Palace by yourself, alright?" Ankhetep furrowed his eyebrows. But Aneksi continued before he could reply. "Listen to me carefully. You are still the Pharaoh and always will be. So, when you return, tell your viziers you want it written for my return. Do this, and I will come to you." Aneksi gently placed a hand on his cheek. "When I am there, we can remember your father and be strong together."

Ankhetep nodded solemnly.

"Okay, Your Highness. I promise I will." Aneksi nodded and leaned over to brush her lips to his forehead. Tears streamed down her cheeks.

"Now, let's see your little sister."

Ankhetep had gone back to the Palace before night fell. He had spent most of the day cradling Azeneth and whispering to her about the secret passageways he frequented when he wanted to run away from his viziers with a promise to show them to her. Kairunamete had watched with them with a nonchalant expression while Aneksi sat beside the two. She could not understand why her father did not seem happy with Ankhetep on good terms with his half-sister.

After Ankhetep had gone and the candles were dimmed in Aneksi's chamber, Kairunamete approached her as the servants settled her in. Aneksi's hair was brushed and it was clear that in the last few months it had become richer and darker now that it reached her chest. Azeneth was sleeping down the hall, where the wet nurse and the three servants from the Temple of Tawaret watched her all night.

"Your return to the Palace will endanger your life as well as Azeneth's," he said, taking a seat by the bed.

"What do you mean?" Aneksi asked, shaking her head. "I thought returning to the Palace was what was best."

Kairunamete paused, looking to find a gentle way to tell her what he was trying to say.

"She was born when her father was dead, Aneksi. Azeneth's legitimacy is easy to embellish." He watched Aneksi look away, the candlelight above her flickering in her moistened eyes. But Kairunamete forged on. "Even returning as the previous Great Royal Wife will not secure your lives when there is a new Pharaoh sitting upon the throne. Those who wish you gone surround him, and you know this. Aneksi, your place in the Palace is fraught."

"Then what am I to do? Stay here?"

He shook his head. "I wish I could keep you here, but that would only make matters worse. However, I do know of one way you can keep Azeneth safe."

Aneksi turned back to her father. "And what's that?"

"You'll have to marry the young boy," Kairunamete said slowly. Aneksi's jaw twitched.

"What?"

Her father cleared his throat.

"Yes, you must become Great Royal Wife for a second time. It's not unprecedented and there is no doubt that this is the only way to keep Azeneth away from the rumors of illegitimacy if her namesake and birthright are so high."

Aneksi covered her mouth with her hand, tears streaming down her cheeks. How could she even think to do such a thing?

"...I informed one of the boy's viziers of this already. I see no reason to truly object to this, Aneksi."

"Please, Father, don't do this to me," Aneksi shut her eyes, bringing her knees to her chest. "I cannot marry his son."

"Aneksi, I loved the Pharaoh as if he were my son- of course it aches me to ask this of you. But wouldn't he want to see his Azeneth grow up? Wouldn't he want her to live in the Palace where she deserves? Is that not the life you want for your daughter?" Aneksi opened her eyes, feeling her chest being torn by her father's words. "Even if Azeneth's protection is written into law, Ankhetep is just a boy. He has years before the words from his lips are responded to with submission. Do you truly want to show the gods you are capable of being a leader, Aneksi? Or was it just a whim that you accepted the title as Great Royal Wife? Aneksi, you have only two choices: stand up or turn back."

PART XXXVII.

"Father, I won't. I won't." Aneksi stared hard at her father's shadowed face, her tears still threatening to fall. "Ankhetep is the Pharaoh's son. I see him as *my* son, Father. How could you send word for this arrangement without having consulted me in the slightest?"

"Look here-"

"No," she cut him off, shaking her head. "I always believed you had my best interest in mind, but it must end now. I married the Pharaoh because I love him with everything in me. I swear by the gods I will not mar-"

"Enough!" Kairunamete shouted. Aneksi jumped in her

seat, wide-eyed and a hand on her chest. "Your naivety is what got us into this ordeal," he snapped. "Have you forgotten that?" Aneksi inhaled sharply at the accusation. "The Pharaoh is dead because he sustained a wound by that slave of yours. A slave you forced into the Palace!"

"Yet she named you as a reason for why she acted as she did!" Aneksi shouted back. Kairunamete pulled back, eyebrows furrowed.

"What did you say?"

Aneksi swallowed. "She said you forced yourself upon her. It's haunted her for this long and she did this all in revenge."

"I..." she watched her father adjust his headpiece and eyes dart from one place to another. "I've done no such thing," he said firmly. "I would never belittle the name of this temple for a slave girl." Aneksi frowned as Kairunamete changed the subject. "Tomorrow morning I'll send you off to the Palace with Azeneth. When I'm called there, it had better be for the crowning of a Great Royal Wife." Aneksi opened her mouth to object but her father had already stood up and turned to go. She watched him walk towards the door -opened by a servant holding a candle- and pause. "You must be careful when you return the Palace," he said over his shoulder.

Aneksi sighed when her father left her chamber. She remained sitting upright, thinking. She could easily do as her father wished; after all, Ankhetep was a child who knew nothing about marriage or of romantic love. He would not doubt Aneksi if she said their marriage was simply a lawful procedure to ensure her title as Great Royal Wife stayed as it was. Aneksi hid her face in her hands.

No. Ankhetep deserved a Great Royal Wife he would grow up to love. And Aneksi would never be that woman, not in that sense. There had to be someone else her father would agree to...with another sigh, Aneksi laid herself down.

She watched some of the older servants finish their work when a thought struck her. Aneksi knew that these women and their families had served, and would serve, her father for all their lives. Surely, they would know everything that occurred within the Temple.

Aneksi sat back up.

"Come here, please," she called out to the two women. They approached Aneksi with bowed heads. "Do you remember Lithra? My slave from across the sea?" The servants shared a brief look and nodded. Aneksi swallowed hard before she opened her mouth to speak. "Then what I said to my father; is it true?" Aneksi felt her heart begin to beat loudly in anticipation of their answer.

The women pursed their lips, eyes set on the floor.

"What exactly did you say?" one of them asked innocently.

"You heard what I spoke about with my father," Aneksi insisted, gazing from one woman to the other. "I know you overheard us. So, tell me: is the accusation true? Did he actually force himself on Lithra?"

The two bit their lip and glanced at each other. Aneksi stared hard at them. She knew Lithra had never liked her father, but she expected such a feeling as most of the slaves here seemed to hold a dislike for him.

"Why do you delay? Is it because he's guilty?"

The women fidgeted in their spot. The gaze would not settle nor meet Aneksi's.

"By Ma'at, answer me!" Aneksi demanded.

"Yes!" one of the two said, wincing. Aneksi felt the air in her lungs leave her. Her hand curled into a fist as the same woman continued, gripping her forearms. "The Lady found out and it ruined her. Any of us would say that is the reason she got so sick–" the servant was cut off by an elbow jab and a warning look from the servant beside her.

Aneksi blinked rapidly. 'The Lady'? Did they mean her

mother? The last time her mother had not been in the Afterlife was a decade ago. That would mean-

"How old was Lithra?" Aneksi asked, wide-eyed. The two turned away from Aneksi slightly, closing their eyes. "How old was she!"

"Please!" one of the women begged.

"We cannot say anymore!" the other cried out. "If the Master finds out, we'll be killed!"

Aneksi forced herself to turn away from them, trying to breathe. It could not be so. She settled into the bed, hugging the sheets around her. Oh gods, she thought, Lithra was only slightly older than she was. How could her father do such a thing to someone? It was then another thought struck Aneksi. She knew her mother had died with secrets and pain- was that secret and pain derived from this event? Was that why her mother had told her to treat Lithra kindly? While her mother died in agony knowing what had happened to Lithra, Lithra lived the same agony every day for the rest of her life.

Aneksi shut her eyes. And the Pharaoh; he was the only other man Lithra knew. She had forced Lithra to know him, befriend him, all the while thinking she had fallen in love with someone else entirely. Who could have imagined that the Pharaoh had stolen both their hearts?

He was also the same man who was gone forever.

Aneksi muffled a sob. Her fists were clenched around the bedsheets and her legs curled into her stomach. She and her father both had done this to Lithra. They were the reason Lithra had turned into the monster she was.

PART XXXVIII.

Aneksi and Azeneth were seated together, but two separate palanquins were set for the travel. Her father had said it was a precautionary measure in case anyone was to try to come after her and the princess. With two palanquins, the criminal would be confused as to which of the two they would attack. But Aneksi did not care to think about it; rather she was much more focused on the fact that the Pharaoh would not be there to greet her as she had imagined the reunion in her head the past four months.

The men who carried her walked slowly to keep from disturbing the royal mother and child too much. Aneksi had her eyes closed for most of the journey, and at some point, finally let herself ruin her eye makeup for the fourth time that morning, knowing this time there would be no servant to wash it away and redo it.

Azeneth squirmed in her arms, making a faint cry. Aneksi

opened her red eyes and internally gasped. She quickly grabbed a piece of cloth from the basket beside her and wiped away the globs of black powder and tears that had fallen onto Azeneth's face. Aneksi did not think to wipe her own face, too transfixed at the Pharaoh's daughter -their daughter- sleeping in her arms.

"You belong to your father," Aneksi choked out, her vision blurring with a fresh set of tears. Aneksi shut her eyes again and bent slightly forward, silent sobs wracking her body.

How could she ever live in the Palace without him? How could she live without him? Everything was a constant reminder that she was alone. And innocent Azeneth, she was the best and worst reminder of it all.

It was past midday when Aneksi and Azeneth reached the Palace. Much to Aneksi's surprise, Ahset and Akhara were the ones who greeted them.

"You look awful," Akhara said as Aneksi passed her daughter to one of the servants from the Temple of Tawaret that had come with her. Aneksi only guessed it was her knowing that the younger of the two half-sisters was the more outspoken one.

"She means to say your feelings have overwhelmed your

appearance. Natural of course," Ahset corrected.

Aneksi exhaled through her nostrils. She was wasting her time and breath on these women. Aneksi desperately needed to visit the Pharaoh's tomb. She glanced at the servant gently rocking Azeneth, and then back at the two consorts. But she needed Azeneth safe first.

"Oh, you must be wondering why we have not left despite the trial's outcome," Akhara said. "Our late husband fell ill too soon to have the law put into effect." Aneksi furrowed her eyebrows, narrowing her eyes as well.

"I'm tired from my trip and my daughter needs seeing to. Thank you for welcoming me in but move aside now."

"Oh yes, your daughter," Akhara said, emphasizing the word 'daughter.' "A shame you did not have a son. A waste, really, now that our husband is gone. Oh, how do you stand it, coming back with a princess and not a prince."

At this, Aneksi felt her blood boil.

"Get. Out. Of. My. Way," Aneksi hissed. "If you say so much another word about my daughter I will send you back to the Temple of Horus faster than any of the Pharaoh's visits to your bedchamber." The two women blinked, completely stunned. The servant beside Anekis turned her head away to suppress her shocked amusement. Aneksi wiped at the remnants of her makeup with her palm in an instinctive manner as she turned away. "Guards, take me to my chambers. Now."

Rai was standing outside what used to be the Pharaoh's private chamber, awaiting Aneksi's return. His usual bronze chest plate was now more than half gold and his simple bronze helmet was replaced with a towering headdress.

Aneksi found her mouth curving into a smile at the sight of her personal guard. But her smile quickly faltered. The Pharaoh was the reason why she trusted Rai so much. It was him who sent the guard on a covert mission to find and rescue her, resulting in their meeting.

Azeneth began to cry by the time Aneksi reached him. The servant from the Temple of Tawaret quickly hushed the child, patting her back, and with a nod from Aneksi, was escorted to the Nursery by the Palace guards.

Rai bowed fully to her when Aneksi returned her attention to him.

"I'm glad to see you were not eased of your service here while I was away," Aneksi said in a low voice. Rai stood upright and flashed a smile in recognition of her honest concern.

"Lady Meryt will be available soon, too, Your Highness."

Aneksi nodded. Rai turned a bit and opened the chamber door. "Please allow me to take you inside and rest, Your Highness-"

Aneksi shook her head.

"No, Rai, I don't have time for rest. I need you to take me to his tomb."

Rai opened his mouth and then closed it, just as he did the door.

"It's been sealed off already, Your Highness, but I will take you there."

Aneksi followed Rai closely, feeling her heart thunder within her breast. How it ached knowing this was how she was meeting the Pharaoh. There would be no final goodbye, no words of optimism. She would not be able to even see or speak or hear or touch him, one last time.

They had not even gone past the hall when Aneksi crumpled to the ground, sobbing.

Rai jumped to her aid, wrapping an arm around her back and slipping one below her knees. A servant carrying two baskets of clothes stopped walking and hunched with her head bowed at the sight of the fallen Queen.

"It's alright, Your Highness, it's not necessary to do so right now," Rai said as he gently lifted Aneksi before her white cotton dress she wore was ruined any further.

"Please check on Azeneth," Aneksi whispered into his neck. She felt him nod and allowed herself to close her eyes as he took her back. Another time, she assured herself. Another time she would go. But right now, the cracks of her heart were still too raw to be mended.

Meryt arrived with Ankhetep later that evening. Meryt hoped that if Aneksi spent time alone in the place she held her most cherished moments with the Pharaoh, it would ease her into a reprieve. But their private chamber seemed to only have broken her further. Memories of the Pharaoh, echoes of his voice and ghost touches were etched into the pristine sheets and mosaic walls.

Aneksi could barely breathe, suffocated by her thoughts and the rising hurt in her chest. She clutched herself, tangled in a mess of pillows and flower petals and cool sheets. That which should have calmed her only brought her to sink farther. The thought of the Pharaoh around her, yet not, nor would he ever be, gave the certainty that he was truly gone. It was a feeling unbeknownst to anything she had ever felt before. Heartbreak; it was the pain with no cure.

Perhaps this was what her mother felt in her last days.

Ankhetep was quiet as he climbed onto the bed. Aneksi

took no heed of him as he curled beside her.

"She'll do no good here," Meryt said to Rai as they watched the two mourn silently. He nodded gravely. "Learning of the Pharaoh's passing so soon after giving birth must have altered her state of mind."

"What can we do, Lady Meryt? Besides Her Highness' life, Princess Azeneth's life is at stake as well."

"Yes, I am aware." Meryt curled a stray lock of hair behind her ear. "Her daughter poses no threat to either His Majesty or the baby Prince Ka-Rae, but it only weakens Her Highness' position...gods." Meryt shook her head, frowning. "The Palace may no longer be a place for Her Highness, but we should find a way to keep Princess Azeneth here."

"Is there a chance Her Regency Lady Kiya will help?" Rai prompted. Meryt glanced at him, eyebrows raised.

"By Ma'at, she just might. She's told me the only thing that pitted her against Her Highness was the worry for her son's life in a political war for the throne. But with Her Highness having a daughter and no chance for a male child, Lady Kiya has nothing to worry about." Meryt paused. "I'll inform Her Highness of her best options when her mind is clear."

"Very well." Rai nodded again.

"I'll at least indulge myself to be of some use to my friend. Bring that tray of herbal drinks here."

After a time, Aneksi brought herself to sit upright. She did not notice Meryt swirling a cup of hot liquid behind her. Aneksi's lips twitched in an effort to smile down at Ankhetep as she placed a hand on his shoulder.

"How are you, Ankhetep?" Aneksi's voice was low. He stared up at her.

"I'm doing my best," he said earnestly. "But Your Highness shouldn't worry about me, I'm a strong young man. My mother believes so." Aneksi nodded.

"Of course. How is she, your mother?"

"She weeps at night as you have done now," Ankhetep answered. Aneksi's shoulders slumped at his words. Ankhetep pinched the bridge of his nose and sighed deeply. "Everyone weeps, and I don't know how to make anyone happy again. I wonder, does that mean I have failed in being the next Pharaoh?"

"Of course not...." Aneksi trailed off. She did not have it in her to cheer the boy up.

"Grieving helps, Your Majesty," Meryt said from behind them. Aneksi's eyes widened at the sound of Meryt and watched the granddaughter of the Temple of Sekhmet walk over with a painted glass cup in hand. "It helps the gods know you have accepted their actions." Ankhetep nodded at this statement while Aneksi hung her head. "Your Highness, this is a stress-relieving tea. Please drink it, for your sake."

Aneksi gratefully took it and looked up at Meryt.

"My daughter, Azeneth; how is she? Do you know what will happen to her?"

Meryt hesitated. "We can talk about this later."

"I want to know!" Ankhetep burst out, leaning forward. "Allow me to help Princess Azeneth, too, Lady Meryt."

Meryt sat at the edge of the bed.

"Alright then, Your Majesty, I'll explain this matter openly to you. But this is very, very important. It will not be an easy problem to handle. Are you ready for that, Your Majesty?"

Ankhetep sat up straighter, puffing his chest.

"Yes, Lady Meryt, for Princess Azeneth I am."

Meryt nodded and glanced at Aneksi. "Then allow me to explain: Her Highness only came to the Palace because she married your father and was crowned Great Royal Wife. But your father rests with the gods now, so Her Highness no longer has a place in the Palace anymore."

"How so? Her Highness still has the title of Great Royal

270

Wife," Ankhetep said.

"That may be, but your mother currently fills that position as she's your Regent."

"Oh."

"This is why Her Highness must seek a place for Princess Azeneth," Meryt continued. "If Her Highness does not have a proper place in the Palace, neither does the Princess. Right now, we'll have to talk to your mother about how to solve this. Will you go now and tell her to call for an audience with Her Highness and myself whenever she is ready?"

Ankehtep nodded. Before he stepped off the bed, he turned to Aneksi.

"I promise to keep my sister safe, Your Highness."

PART XXXIX

Kiya sat back into her throne, a few fingers cast across her face as she leaned on her right elbow. She was wearing a sleeveless blue linen dress, her neck, waist, and arms fitted with carved gold. The white, blue and gold paints and powder around her eyes did well to distract one from noticing the burst blood vessels of her eyes from her constant crying. But the most noticeable of all was the giant scarab amulet hanging loosely around her throat.

The throne to her right was empty.

"Only a day has passed since your arrival and you seek something from me already," Kiya said with a roll of her eyes. "What is it?"

Aneksi, dressed in a plain white dress and sparse jewelry, sank to her knees, her hands clasped together. Kiya dropped her hand away from her face at Aneksi's sign of desperation.

"Please, Your Regency, I've lost so much already. Our husband, my son...I beg you to keep my daughter away from this fate."

Kiya's jaw twitched.

"I will not have you or your daughter interfere with this succession."

"By Ma'at, I don't want to either," Aneksi pleaded. "All of this warring has only brought suffering to me."

"Then why have you come back, Your Highness. If dealing with these affairs only afflict you."

Aneksi sighed, lowering her hands to her lap. "Azeneth deserves to be living in this Palace with her kinsmen. Raising her away from her lineage would be wrong of me."

"Azeneth? Hmm." Kiya's eyes briefly met Aneksi's. "Does the Lord-Priest know you are here, groveling at my feet, for the safety of a mere princess?"

"I've always tried to please him. It cost me everything," Aneksi whispered. Her gaze lowered to the base of the throne. She stared at the dark grey and pink veins in the marble, her eyes watering. "Azeneth may be one of six sitting princesses, but she matters to me." She would have mattered to her father.

Kiya looked away, once more rolling her eyes.

"Your pitiful state unnerves me. Lady Meryt, make her stand." Meryt did as Kiya instructed. "Good." She paused. "I have a proposition for you and your little Azeneth. If you accept, you are telling me the Lord-Priest will adhere to what I have to say with no objections. If he makes any indication of going back on it, I'll nullify my offer completely. Do you understand that?" Aneksi nodded in earnest. Meryt closed her eyes briefly in hope. "Alright then. I'll agree to have your daughter wed my Prince Ka-Rae if you agree to live away from the Palace from their betrothal henceforth. In addition, you'll not attempt to regain any sort of position here so long as you live."

Aneksi felt her blood go cold at the conditions of her scheme. Beside her, Meryt stiffened. After a moment of stunned silence, Aneksi spluttered, "So this...marriage will promise Azeneth's safety in the Palace?"

Kiya gave a short laugh, devoid of any amusement, and sat up, lowering her forearms on the armrest.

"Between two mothers, yes, that will be its purpose. But between two consorts, there are no guarantees."

Aneksi looked at Meryt. Her friend gave a half shrug, but also an encouraging smile. Aneksi's lip quivered. Azeneth would not know her mother, but at least she would be alive.

"Why must I be away from her?" Aneksi asked, turning back to Kiya. The Regent raised a leg to cross it over the other. Her dark eyes met Aneksi's hazel ones.

"You remind me of all that went wrong in my life." Aneksi held Kiya's gaze before dropping it. "So, what's your decision, Your Highness?" Kiya quipped. "The faster you decide, the faster I'll secure your Azeneth's position."

Aneksi inhaled sharply. This was it. Azeneth marrying Ka-Rae ensured that she would not ascend to the throne as Kiya wanted, but also meant she would be protected by the Temple of Isis as Aneksi wanted. The only downfall was that she would be living alone and away from her daughter for the rest of their lives.

"I'm waiting."

Aneksi sighed. There was no hope for her anyway. Azeneth would have to be the Tri-God Temple's bearer from now on. Until the day came for Azeneth to play her part, her father would have to bide his time.

"I agree to these terms and I know my father will as well."

Kiya once more sat back into her throne. Her eyes darted to her right. "Good. It will occur in due time. Guards, take them away."

Aneksi refused to go back to the private chamber and instead, returned to her consort chamber. Meryt bowed her head in farewell, as she was due in the medicinal chambers. Aneksi laid herself down on the sofa and closed her eyes.

"How did it happen?" she whispered. Rai, standing at the doorway, cocked his head.

"Your Highness?"

"How did the Pharaoh...?"

Rai nodded to himself and kept his eyes on the floor. "It was all very quick. None of the physicians -even Lady Meryt, or the apprentice- were allowed to treat him once His Majesty was taken underground. As far as I know, the viziers and High Priests Ekmati and Kahorus conducted everything."

Aneksi curled into herself. Why did the gods do this to her? They had taken everything from her. Lithra, her twins, the love of her life, and what little friends she had made in the Palace- Meryt and Rai.

She had everything when she first came here. And now she had nothing.

PART XL.

News of Princess Azeneth and Prince Ka-Rae's engagement was met with an enormous appeal from the viziers. Especially as it signaled an end for the Tri-God Temple's reach for the throne for two generations.

Aneksi was torn between wanting to spend every moment of her last week with Azeneth and wanting to distance herself from the inevitable. Eventually, she made the decision to spend only her last night in the Palace with Azeneth and spend the remaining six days writing a letter addressed to the baby princess for each day she did not visit her. And while Aneksi had grown up without many fond memories of her own mother, she was adamant about ensuring Azeneth knew her mother in the best light. She hoped the letters would keep Azeneth on the right path.

When her father arrived for the engagement, Aneksi could not find it in herself to speak or remain in the same chamber as he was. The truth behind his actions against Lithra was still fresh in her mind. But she could not avoid his company forever.

The betrothal ceremony was kept small despite the affair being well-known to the public. Aneksi and her father sat opposite of Kiya and the High Priest of Isis while two servants from the Nursery did their best to keep the Azeneth and Ka-Rae from crying too much. The viziers remained in the back of the portico with the Royal Scribe noting the entirety of the agreement.

A table was brought in holding celebratory food between the two families and the servants even managed to put up colored banners along the wall.

It was all over in a half hour.

"I understand this will bind our Temples for a time," Kairunamete said after the Royal Scribe had set away his inks. "Done so graciously by Her Regency." Kiya inclined her head at the compliment.

"Yes; what is yours is now mine to protect. This betrothal is but a single event that will introduce you to how things will run with my son as Pharaoh." Aneksi's eyes widened at Kiya's words. *An iron fist and an open heart.* Could Ankhetep have begged Kiya to find a way to keep Azeneth safe?

"The Temple of Isis will see to it that it stays this way," her father added, breaking Aneksi from her thoughts.

"Oh, of course," Kairunamete said dryly. "We'll see how

that plays out."

Aneksi glanced fearfully from her father to the High Priest of Isis. Her father needed to be careful about how he spoke to the ruling Temple from now on. Azeneth's safety was at stake.

But to her slight relief, Isiskah laughed at her father's words. And just like his daughter's, the laugh was devoid of mirth and was rather more of a show of power over the situation.

"That we will, Lord-Priest, that we will."

After this, the two families split ways. Aneksi began following the servants to visit the Nursery when her father grabbed her arm. Aneksi flinched and her father quickly withdrew his hand.

"I have some news that you must know, Aneksi," he said in a low voice. "Come walk for a bit. And tell that guard of yours to step back." Aneksi glanced at Rai, who met her gaze and did as her father said. Aneksi pressed her palms to her elbows and stood a distance apart from her father. He did not take note of it. "The circumstances are not so bad for the time being," Kiarunamete said, folding his hands behind his back. "But, as it should be expected, I am in the motion of reclaiming what we lost. I recently married again-"

Aneksi stopped walking, staring at her father obliviously walked on a few more steps before realizing it.

"I have a new mother? When did this happen?"

Kairunamete rolled his eyes and waved a hand in the air in annoyance.

"Yes, lawfully she is now your mother. But that is beside the point, Aneksi!" His voice now bordered on excitement. "The importance of this matter is that she will be soon giving birth. If the gods do aid us in our plight, we will be graced with an eligible daughter to marry the boy Pharaoh or a son who will continue as the next Lord-Priest of the Tri-God Temple. Or both, however many children she bears."

Aneksi could not be for sure what part of his 'news' she abhorred the most, the fact that her father had remarried in secret or that she would be an older sister to any of that woman's children who were no more than just products of her father's behest. She felt her stomach twist.

Why did such motives settle so strangely within her? This was how things worked. How noblemen survived and maintained their station. A life of politics. It was becoming clearer that it was one Aneksi was never meant for. After all, her father's information should have brought optimism if she were, not repugnance.

"Aneksi, Aneksi! You're grown, so handle this, will you," Kairunamete said, the annoyance in his voice returning. "As my daughter, I've provided you with all the comfort that I can. But there is so much I can provide for so long. I'm now investing in the future of another, with aspirations as great as yours once were."

"I understand what you're saying," Aneksi began, but the Lord-Priest shook his head.

"No my dear Aneksi, I'm telling you now that once you leave this Palace, my ties with you will also be cut." Aneksi froze. "But, don't mistake this: I still hold you close and will fight that you continue living in comfort. It's simply now your turn to help yourself."

"F-father?" Aneksi stuttered, tears pricking her eyes. Had he always been like this? His expression did not change.

"Go spend your remaining time with Azeneth. I'll look after her once you are gone, so there is no need to have you worked up over such matters." Kairunamete stepped forward to lightly graze his lips on Aneksi's forehead before brushing past her.

Aneksi stayed frozen in her position, staring at the empty hallway.

"This way, Your Highness," she heard Rai say feeling his

hand hover below her left elbow. With his other arm, he indicated in the direction to the Nursery. Aneksi nodded once and forced her legs forward.

Aneksi's distress melted away once Azeneth was placed into her arms. She sat down on the red and white bench seat lined against the painted wall and let time take its course. Just once, Azeneth's eyes shuttered open for a few seconds. Aneksi felt her chest swell at Azeneth's blinking eyes and little head movements.

"She's awake!" Aneksi cried out, looking about to tell someone. "Rai, she's awake!" Her personal guard leaned over, capturing Azeneth's attention.

Rai bowed to the baby. "Your Highness."

Aneksi beamed in pride at her little girl. Azeneth yawned and her dark eyes shifted around. Aneksi bent forward to kiss the girl's nose and forehead.

"I love you, Azeneth."

Aneksi's last meal was a formal dinner in the Palace. Ankhetep sat where his father once did, with Kiya sitting beside him. Aneksi sat below them with the other consorts. The Master of Servants made his routine announcements, but this time ending with Ankhetep's name, and the meal commenced.

Aneksi did not eat much, feeling rather dissatisfied with everything. After the meal, Meryt suggested they bathe in the hot spring to raise Aneksi's mood.

Without the heat of the sun above them, the waters had cooled. The surface was now a dark violet mirror littered with the reflection of the ever-shifting fire from the standing torches. But sinking into it, Aneksi felt no better.

"Meryt, may I ask a favor from you?" she asked. Meryt looked over from where she sat, a servant rubbing castor and almond oil into her short, black curls.

"Yes, of course. What is it?"

"I know my father will ensure no harm comes to Azeneth...but will you promise me that she will be loved?" Aneksi felt her voice crack.

"Lady Aneksi..."

"Meryt, I want her to know there is more to life than the enemies she will make for simply being who she is," Aneksi continued in a low voice, her gaze set on the dark water rippling in front of her. "For who her mother is."

Meryt nodded. Aneksi finally looked up at her.

"On her seventh birthday, I want you to give her the letters I wrote for her. Meryt, I want you to guide her and Rai to guard her–"

Meryt moved away from the servant to embrace Aneksi. She closed her eyes as Aneksi clutched her, sobbing.

"By Ma'at, I swear it."

FINALE

It was in the outskirts of town, behind the great walls of the Palace, where the mud-brick buildings and houses were known for crumbling every so often. The dust never settled here, and the sun never gave up. Crops were long forgotten and instead, the village bore craftsmen and artisans with meager earnings and dreams so profound one would think any day now, the gods would grant it.

Aneksi had relocated here and lived among the barefooted children and humble people for the past eight years. A few days after arriving, Aneksi had declined the village potter's offer for marriage and she now slept alongside his wife and children in the back chamber of the house.

Once or twice life would be forced into an enticing fright when a passing nobleman sped by or a thief came for bread. Aneksi's hands had lost all their former softness from meddling with clay all day and her arms, shoulders, and feet had deepened in color. Her hair was all but what covered her scalp- the majority cut off and made into a wig left to stand in her shared chamber, while she routinely cut away any growing locks.

"Be careful!" Aneksi wrenched the two children into the air as they ran. They squirmed in her grasp and Aneksi set them down with a grunt. The children -two young boys- turned to look at her. "Your father broke a jar this morning. I've yet to sweep everything up." They gazed at the shattered remnants of the pottery and made a leap over the broken bits. Aneksi gasped and reached a hand out to catch them but did not need to. They had made it to the other side of the outside shed without harm.

Aneksi sighed and grabbed the reed broom and quickly finished the task before any of the other children ran this way. With this finished, she placed the broom back into the corner of the shed. Aneksi then turned to the adjoined kitchen where Ebio, the children's mother, stroked the flames to keep the pot above it boiling with her youngest on her hip.

"Those rascals," she said, in a mix of scorn and affection. "Here, take her," she continued, offering Aneksi the baby.

Aneksi took the child into her arms and bounced on the heels of her feet to keep her calm. Ebio went over to the square hole dug in the ground where they preserved their food and retrieved the last pieces of salted duck meat.

"Nefere, can you run over to the tradesman's and see how much of his salted poultry he's willing to give for the usual?" Aneksi nodded. "Oh, and take the boys with you. There, I'll take her from you," Ebio once more lifted her baby in her arms.

Aneksi quickly set herself to calling for the Ebio's sons. They came running from behind the house holding a dead snake outstretched between them.

"Were either of you bitten?" Aneksi frantically asked, looking over their arms and necks. They shrugged.

"You worry too much, Nefere," the elder of the boys said. "Right, Unn?" His younger brother nodded.

"I worry so much because neither of you will!" Aneksi said, crossing her arms across her chest. "But good work, you two. Your mother wants me to take you to the tradesman. We can see if he'll trade that snake in for something nice to eat." The boys jumped up and down, grinning from ear to ear at the thought of contributing so beneficially to their family. "Come on now. We need to go."

The tradesman lived in his storehouse farther out of the village with a servant of his who did most, if not all, of the stocking and orders in the back. The servant was maimed -a useless left arm and a bad knee- which was why the tradesman trusted him to not run off with anything.

Unn's older brother elbowed him as they walked towards the storehouse. The younger boy turned his head to Aneksi.

"Nefere, can you tell us about your past?"

"What do you want to know," Aneksi replied.

It always struck a sensitive spot in her chest at the thought of recalling life before this town, but Aneksi had gotten used to the idea of giving vague stories about it. Ebio had once asked if she had ever been married before coming to the town, but after seeing Aneksi's face at the question, Ebio never brought the topic back up.

"Were you rich?" Unn asked. Aneksi glanced down at the boy. "Kamu says the jewels are yours-"

"Unn!" his older brother slapped his arm.

Aneksi froze. "You found them?"

"I knew they were real!" Kamu shouted, letting go of his end of the snake to dance about. "We'll be rich! I bet we could buy everything the tradesman has with just one of them!"

Aneksi was breathing hard now. "Lower your voice, Kamu!"

"Why?" Kamu said, stopping mid-dance to place his fists on his hips. "I want to eat more than once a day, Nefere! I bet you know what that feels like since you had all those expensive things hidden away!"

"I..." Aneksi felt her throat close. Before she left the Palace for good, Meryt had managed to stash away Aneksi's wedding jewelry into her belongings. Aneksi buried them in their backyard the night she was taken in by the potter.

"What's all this about jewels I hear?" the tradesman said from the doorway of his storehouse.

The tradesman was ancient-looking, with all the dunes of a desert carved in his face, but it only fooled a newcomer into thinking his age had the best of him.

"Just wishes of fortune," Aneksi quickly answered as the boys ran up to the tradesman, who allowed them in.

Once the three were all inside, the tradesman shut the door and stood there. There were no windows or other doors in the storehouse. Just the main one so the tradesman could make sure nothing was pickpocketed.

"I'm going to find the best weapon and be a mighty warrior!" Kamu declared. "And the finest goblets for mother and father to drink from!"

"Me too!" Unn followed after his brother to the back of the storehouse where all the more precious items were.

"The usual, I assume," the tradesman said. Aneksi

nodded. Before going over to retrieve the dried meats, the tradesman frowned. "Tell Weser I want more creative designs this time. They've become tasteless now."

Aneksi nodded again. "I'll let him know. Also, the boys have a snake with them."

The tradesman's eyes lit up. "Poisonous, perhaps? I have a few requests for it."

Aneksi gave him a tight-lipped smile. There would never be a time there would not be a demand for those toxins. She knew that well.

"I didn't check. I'll get the boys over, so you may have a look." The tradesman nodded and made a motion with his hand to shoo her in the direction of where the boys were.

Aneksi walked to the back and weaved around the heavy hanging rugs. To her left, she saw Kamu and Unn touching the hilt of a rusted dagger. To her right, she caught sight of the tradesman's servant's back as he carried one of the potter's larger creations with his good arm.

His gait was off; he dragged one of his feet as he did so. She watched him struggle a bit, feeling sorry for him. There was not much a one-armed man could do to survive. But she also watched him in curiosity.

What did his face look like? What was his name?

Realizing she had been staring, Aneksi turned away to catch sight of something she had not seen in the storehouse before. On the wall next to the servant was a painting- of two young rulers sitting on the throne. They were too captivated by the other's eyes to have noticed that the painter had immortalized their moment together.

Aneksi blinked a few times and wiped the edges of her eyes, forcing herself to look away. She walked over to Kamu and Unn and bent down to place her hands on their shoulders.

"Boys, your mother is waiting for us, remember? Show the tradesman the snake you brought, and we can return home with something for her."

"Fine!" Kamu snapped and did not hesitate to add, "But we'd better buy something for us next time!" before the two ran ahead to deal with the tradesman.

Aneksi sighed. She should have planned for something like this to happen. After all, it was only a matter of time before she slipped up. Aneksi straightened and glanced back at the servant. He was standing in front of the painting.

For the first time in the eight years Aneksi had been here, she stood face-to-face with him. She struggled to breathe under his gaze. Aneksi took a step forward, a hand half outstretched, and mouth open, but no sound escaped her throat.

"Neferkempi? My beautiful storm, is it really you?"

Made in the USA
Middletown, DE
21 January 2020